There are Two faces t
By: Robert E. Schofi

There are Two Faces to Every Story Copyright © 2015 by Robert Schofield

All Rights reserved. No part of this book may be reproduced in any form or by any electronic or mechanical means, including information storage and retrieval systems, without permission in writing from the author and/or publisher, except by a reviewer who may quote brief passages in a review.

This book is a work of fiction. Names, places, characters, and/or incidents are a product of my imagination or used fictitiously. Any resemblance to any actual person (living or dead), events, or locals is entirely coincidental.

ISBN-13: 978-1519316271
ISBN-10: 1519316275

List of Completed Novels and Short Stories that are available for sell by: Robert Schofield

The New America Series:
1st: A Hunter's Diary

The Evolution Series:
The Experimental Outbreak (Short Story/ Prologue to the Series)
1st: Chaos

Harley and Easton Short Story Series:
1st: The Ghost of Cindy Baker
2nd: The Unknown Robber'

Independent Novels:
There are Two Faces to Every Story

Acknowledgments....

First I want to give thanks to God because without him none of this would have been possible.

I want to thank my loving finance, Destiny, for always being there and supporting my decisions. Without your support and helping me stay on track I don't know if I ever would have finished.

I want to thank my mother and father for always standing behind my decisions even when I was a pain in the ass.

I would like to thank my sister, Emily, for being as unusual as me and understanding a point that I was trying to get at when most people wouldn't.

I also would like to thank CreateSpace.com for giving me the option of self-publishing. Without their website this book would have never became a reality. So, thank you so much.

I want to give thanks to my three sons, Pearson, Parker, and Rilie. Without seeing you boys grow up I don't know if I would have ever had the motivation to write this book.

The last group of people I want to give thanks to is you the reader. If it was not for you reading and enjoying a piece of my mind, then I would not have a book being published at all. So thank you from the deepest part of my heart and I have you enjoy reading There are Two Faces to Every Story.

This book is for my loving mother, Sarah. I know that I am a pain in the ass 99% of the time, but know that I love you. And thank you for teaching me the many lessons that you have taught me over the years.

~*Prologue*~

I PULL INTO the driveway after work. I work at the police department in Chicago, Illinois. Being here in this city is a nerve racking job with all of the killings and gang wars that take place. My wife, Shyanne Gibbs, warns me every morning before I go to work. She tells me to be very careful because she knows that one wrong move could be my last.

"When are you going to give up this job and go to a safer job?" I can hear her asking over and over again.

"When I find something that pays me just as good as this job," I would always respond back.

Usually at the end of the sentence the conversation ends because she knows that I am right. Between our mortgage of our nice house to the two car payments we have.

I drive a blue F-150 extended cab. Shyanne; though has a complete different taste in vehicles all together. I like trucks and jeeps that I can get dirty in the mud in my spare time. My wife though she likes the expensive luxury cars. That would be the reason why there is a dark red (almost a blood red color) Mercedes Benz that is parked in the garage as well.

I reach my right arm up and hit the button that is located

on my sun visor. Seconds later the garage door starts to creep open. When the door reaches the top, I let off the brake and my truck begins to move forward. After I make sure the tail end of my truck is fully inside the garage I hit the brake again. I then place my truck into park and shut off the engine. I open the drivers door and step out. I walk into my unlocked house and close the door behind me.

Usually when I walk through the door I can hear Shyanne in the kitchen preparing dinner for me. Today though, is different when I walk through the door I hear nothing, but dead silence. I know she is home because her car is here. Now as I open the closest door to put my jacket in it hers is still there as well. She would have never left today without her jacket because it is freezing outside. It is the middle of winter in Chicago, so freezing doesn't quite describe that right.

I close the closest door and walk into the kitchen. When I do she is not in there at all. First thought that comes through my mind is that she is sick and laying down in our bedroom. I immediately turn around and go upstairs. When I reach the top flight of stairs I turn to the left and enter our bedroom.

"Honey, I am home. Are you okay?" I say quietly at first just in case she is asleep.

I get no answer from the other part of the room. I walk through a small area and enter the part of the main bedroom.

"Shyanne are you in..." I say a little louder as I walk into the main part of the bedroom. That is all I get out when I am hit by complete shock.

Well it really was not any shock at all it just was the answer to my question. When I enter the room I noticed my wife laying restless in our bed. I walk over to the side of her and bend down to give her a kiss. I do just that on her forehead, but when my lips meet her head there is something wrong. Her head is cold as ice even though the house is steaming of heat. I pull back her cover and this time I feel the same cold chills that my wife does going down my spine. Through my blue eyes I see a puddle blood and in the middle of it is my wife's body staining our white sheets.

I fall to my knees in shock and grab my phone from my

pocket. I dial 9-1-1 and seconds later a woman's voice comes over the phone.

"What is your emergency?" the woman says.

" My wife," I pause as a tear rolls down my face and then I continue, "She is dead."

~*Chapter 1*~

TWO MONTHS LATER...
    I DRIVE SLOWLY one car behind the hearse that is carrying my wife's dead body. Two months ago my wife was brutally murdered inside our Chicago home. She use to always warn me about how dangerous my job was for my life, but she never thought about how dangerous it was for her.
    My partner detective Al Smith and I before my wife's murder was searching for a man that goes by the name of Scott Frost. Frost is a man (more like a psycho) that we have been looking for; for years. He is wanted for the murders of thirteen people. One of those includes my wife. That is just what we know of course there could be more.
    We had been closing in on Frost since he decided to send a message by murdering my wife. That is part of the reason it has taken so long for us to have the funeral because we the medical examine had to determine whether or not that she was murdered by Frost or someone else. Sure enough he was the one who we believe did it. Either that or he has someone copy catting his murders.
    Frost like to dismember his victims into several pieces. The papers have called him, *The Real American Psycho.* I

hate when newspapers give a serial killer a name because most of the killers get off on this sort of thing. Which usually leads to us detectives having more work to do because there usually are several more bodies to come along with it.

I begin to slow down because the brake lights of the hearse burn bright red through the pouring rain. Finally the hearse followed by my vehicle comes to a complete stop. I see both the drivers and passengers side doors open and two men get out from either side.

When I turn the truck off I hop out of my own car. I feel the cold rough rain pouring down on my body. A few moments later the young woman that was in my passenger seat comes over to me with an umbrella to offer me to get under with her.

The young girl look just like her mother. Her mother is the same person that is riding in the back of the hearse. She has long, curly, blonde hair and beautiful blue eyes. This young woman is my daughter and her name is Sarah Gibbs.

The day that her mother was found dead she had talked to her mother just that morning. She still technically lived with us as she just graduated high school, but she was not home that day. She had been in California for a week touring the University of Stanford. That morning she had called her mother to tell her the great news that she would be attending Stanford in the fall. It was suppose to be one of the happiest days of her young life so far.

When I had called my daughter later on that night she expected it was because I was calling to congratulate her on her success. So, when I gave her the news of her mother's death she was completely hit with surprise. I booked her a flight home immediately. The only thing I can say that is positive is that tomorrow that she will be flying back out to California to start her fall semester.

As Sarah offers the comfort of the umbrella I shake my head to decline the kind offer. She knows that I have been taking the death of her mother very hard. Even though I did not talk about it or say a word to even show that I am hurting.

My wife and I had been married for twenty-five years when this happened. There will be no other woman like her.

A frown comes on my daughter's face as I declined her. I wish that I could just blank out everything and most days I can, but not today. My daughter though needs me to be strong for her. I reach in and give her a kiss on her cheek. I see a small smirk come on her face even though it seems to be sarcastic.

"I will be over there in a second. Make sure you save me a seat," I tell her.

"Okay. I love you."

"I love you, too," I reply.

I watch as my beautiful daughter walks over to my wife's final resting spot. I however though must go to the hearse and help carrying my wife's body.

When I reach the hearse I am met by the two men who got out of the front of the hearse, two of my brother-in-laws, and Shyanne's father. The six of us will be the ones who will be carrying the casket of my wife to her final resting spot.

The driver from the hearse open the back door of the hearse. They grab either side one by one till all of six of us are holding a part of the casket. Once we all have a great grip we begin to walk were all the rest of the ground is located. It is not very far away from where the cars were parked at. I would say about twenty-five yards. We reach the tent that covers all of the guest. When we do we walk through the middle of everyone to the front. As I pass each roll I can see many people from her side of the family that I have only met once. They never called her or came to visit while she was alive. In fact the only time I ever met them was at our wedding so I probably wouldn't even remember their names. Actually I know I don't their names I just know their faces and that is hard to determine because they have aged twenty-five years.

We reach the front of the tent and place the casket on the table by the preacher. The preacher walks over and puts his hand on my shoulder. I turn around and thank the preacher for being there. Then I proceed to my seat in the front roll by Sarah.

~*Chapter 2*~

I TAKE MY SEAT right beside Sarah. As I do so the preacher opens his bible and looks out across the crowd. It is not a very large crowd, but big enough that my wife would be happy on the turn out. My wife was always afraid that no one would attend her funeral when she died.

"You are so silly, Shyanne. You know that you will at least have Sarah and I there no matter what," I would tell her.

She would always roll her eyes and reply by saying, " You two don't count."

My wife in life always tried to help everyone out because she said that the best way to live life is to be known for all the good you do. She is and always will be my angel that prevents me from going overboard.

"Shyanne Gibbs, a loving mother and a wonderful wife," the preacher starts.

He had that right on both of those statements. Shyanne loved our daughter with every inch of her heart. I am surprised she had anything left at all to love me with because she loved our daughter so much. Then him saying about her being a wonderful wife. That is an understatement. She defines the perfect wife. Sure we had our fights, but what couples don't.

"She was a heroic woman to the community as she started up *The American Child Association.*"

The American Child Association is an organization that my wife created for children that are in need. Most of the kids are ones that she found on the streets and since we were fine on money she helped them out. One thing lead to another and soon our police department started bringing in juvenile kids from the streets that messed up. It was in some sort of a way a second chance place. The kicker was the kids could only be in trouble once before and if they screwed up while in the program then they are out. She was able to help a lot of kids with this program, but of course there was the hard-headed kids who didn't take advantage of their second chance. Those kids are the ones who bothered her the most because she couldn't help them. That just was the kind of person she was though.

"Today we will hear from some of Shyanne's loved ones who will described their time with her on this Earth. Now I will hand this spot over to Sarah Gibbs. Mrs. Gibbs daughter," the preacher continues.

I let go of Sarah's hand as she gets up and walks to the front of everyone. When she reaches the spot the preacher grabs her hand and kisses it. He then moves out of the way and my daughter takes his place.

I listen as she tells her memories of her mother. Some made her cry and some of them made the crowd laugh. I kind of tone her out as I have flashbacks of my wife's memories. Then it is my turn to tell my wife's stories.

I walk slowly up to where my daughter is standing. Instead of her walking back to her seat I ask for her to stand up there next to me. At the moment I will need her strength and courage.

I stand staring over everyone trying to build up the words to say something, but I can't. I look around stunned at a loss for words. I look over at my wife's coffin and beside it is a picture of her. I remember when that picture was taken.

It was the year before Sarah was born. We took vacation at Golf Shores and we rented out a beach house. She was out in the ocean when I took the picture from the sand of the ocean. I can't swim so I decide not to go in even in the shallow part.

I flashback to where I was looking at the coffin and then it happens. My eyes fill of water and then overflows. My eyes begin to pour tons and tons of tears that down poured my face. I was suppose to give a speech about my wife, but I couldn't.

My daughter helps me find my seat as we watch them put Shyanne in the ground. My daughter and I watch as everyone leaves. We are the last ones standing before my wife's grave as they begin to fill in the dirt over top of her.

~*Chapter 3*~

A WEEK LATER...

I PARK MY TRUCK in the parking lot across from the station. I make sure I lock it and then begin to walk across the street to a building that reads, *Chicago Police Department.* I walk through the front door.

Instead of taking the elevator I take the steps as I always do.

"Maybe I should change my approach at doing some stuff. Even some things like taking elevator instead of stairs," I say to myself. It was just a thought though.

I reach the third level of the building and walk through the door. Most days I would go to the second floor where my desk is located at, but I was told to see the captain today when I first came in.

There is only two rooms on the entire third floor. There is the room you walk into where there is a brunette at a receptions desk.

"Hey, Tara," I say.

Tara Quinn is the receptionist working for the captain. If you ask me she is doing more than just that for the captain, but that is just my opinion. The first week that the captain took the chair he fired the old receptionist and hired this brunette babe. Every once in a while when no one is coming up to the captains' floor Tara comes out with her hair all messed up. That and when you are on the second floor you can hear consisting banging noises coming from the third floor.

The captain is not married so good for him. There is nothing wrong with it then.

"Hey James. I am sorry for your loss," she says.

"Thank you." I answer and then continue on, "Is the captain in there?"

"Yeah."

If I was anyone else I would have to wait for the captain to say it was okay to come in. Lucky for me though I am who I am. I go straight to the door that reads, *Captain David Green.*

The captain has had his chair for about three years now. He was my former partner before he got the promotion. So we are pretty darn close.

I open the door and go straight in. When I enter the room there is a dark hair, bulky size man sitting behind a desk. He has glasses on as he is reading some paper work it looks like. As soon as I open the door I draw his immediate attention because he knows that I am the only one who just walks straight in.

"James come have a seat," he says as he stands up tall. When I say tall I mean tall. When he stands up straight he is approximately six-foot four inches.

I take his offer as I have a seat in the chair across from him. Before I do though our hands meet to shake. Finally I sit and he does the same. After doing so he takes his glasses off and folds them. He then places them on his desk and folds his hands. Those glasses where only for reading. For some reason he can see everything else perfect except when he goes to read something. I actually find it kind of amusing and tease him about it all the time because I still have twenty-twenty vision.

"I am really sorry about not being about to make it to the funeral. Shyanne was like my sister," he tries to explain.

"It is fine. I know things have been busy around here.

Plus she would understand anyways. She always has with our work," I reply to him.

We sit there for a moment just in silence. I am surprised he hasn't started to say it yet. It doesn't take long though because I see his lips begin to move.

"You know you don't have to come back so fast. You can take a little bit more time to recover," he announces.

"I am ready. Besides me being at home is driving me crazy. I need to get out there and find Frost," I declare.

"Yeah about that. You need to back off a little bit."

I feel the blood rushing to my head and my heart begin to pound faster and harder than normal.

"What!" I exclaim.

"We got so close and he killed Shyanne, James," he tries to explain his reasoning.

I say nothing and walk out of the room. That is what is best because I am pissed. He also knows that when I am ticked off to leave me alone. So that is why he did not try to stop me.

I go back to the stairway and walk down to the second floor where my desk is. I reach my desk and my partner, Al Smith walks up to me.

"Nice to see you back here," he states.

"Not now," I reply strongly.

"Well, I can see you went to see the captain already. Well hopefully this can cheer you up."

I given him a certain look. The one like what the hell do you got in mind.

"I know the captain said leave Frost alone, but..." he declares

"But what?"

"One of my CIs' called me today claiming he seen Frost earlier."

"How long ago?" I say as I stand up from my chair quickly.

"I just got off the phone with them."

"What about captain?" I question.

It is one thing putting my job out there on the line, but detective Smith's is a different story. He is suppose to be doing his job, but with me it is personal. Smith is a good detective and doesn't deserve to lose his job because of me. I taught him everything he knows the past three years that we have been partners so I know he is a good one.

Smith raises his chin and states, "Fuck the captain. This guy killed your wife."

I think about it for a moment and then look at detective Smith.

"Well, lets go get the Son-of-a-bitch," I answer him.

~*Chapter 4*~

WE EXIT THE BUILDING as if we are going for a scroll in a park. We move quietly but quickly to the outside of the building. When we do we walk across the street to the same parking garage where I parked my truck at. Only this time we don't go to my truck that is parked on the sixth level. Instead we stop on the first level and go towards a black Lincoln town-car.

I usually drive, but my mind is so crazy right now it is not the best idea for me to drive. So, I open the passenger side door and hop into the seat. Seconds later the drivers side door the same and Smith sits down. He starts the car and we drive out of the garage.

"So, where did your CI supposedly see a spotting of Frost at?" I question.

"His house."

"We have had that place on lock down for months now. You think of all places he just ran home out of the blue?" I declare.

"I'm just going from the information I was told."

"Then why didn't our officers not call it in?"

"I am not sure," Smith answers.

We drive towards the outer part of the city limits. When we reach the road that we are meant to be at. There is a patrol car park in front of Frost's house. We park behind the squad car. When the car finally comes to a complete stop Smith puts the car into park. I go to get out of the car, but before I can the door locks.

"What are you doing?" I question as I turn around to look at Smith.

"We need to talk first."

"About what? We don't have time for this. Frost could get away."

He doesn't unlock the door so that we can get the man that murdered my wife.

"Are you okay to do this?"

"Of course."

"I am sticking my neck out for you and Shyanne here. I don't care to at all. I just got to know that if Frost is in fact in here that you will do the right thing. I have to know that if we go in there he will be arrested and suffer for his crimes. Instead of you going in there for revenge and end up killing him," Smith states.

"This is about revenge, partner. But I know what it is right. You have my word we will arrest him," I answer.

He facial looks like he is content with my answer. Seconds later before we get out of the car a man appears. He knocks on the drivers side window. Smith rolls down the window. The man must be Smith's CI because you can tell from his look that he is a drug addict. My mother raised me to not judge before I know. I can't help it though because I am so certain he is. From the needle marks in his forearm probably heroin is his choice.

"Is he still in there?"

"Yeah no one has left since he entered."

"Okay. Thank you," Smith says.

The CI ran away in a hurry. Probably to go to the station to get his payment so that he can waste it on more drugs.

"Now can we go in!" I declare.

Smith unlocks the door and I immediately open my door. He follows my lead. I walk up to the squad car in front of us.

I can tell something is wrong right away because the windows are all frosted up. If the cops were in there they would have had the heat on.

I knock on the window anyways. Instead of hearing silence like I expect to I hear a cracking noise coming from inside the car. I try to wipe away some of the frost to see inside, but I can't. The car had been sitting here so long the frost is thick and heavy.

So the next best thing to do is to open the door. I do just that and when I do I am hit with immediate shock. What I see is something from a horror movie. Just like my wife's body the two cops inside the car are completely dismembered. I only know that there is two cops because I looked it up on my lab-top so that I could cuss them out for not calling it in. I kind of feel bad now for wanting to do that since they are dead.

"What is it?" Smith says as he comes around the corner.

He stops right on the spot as he sees the frosted dead corpse. He goes to call it in, but I quickly stop him.

"What the hell?" He yells.

"If you call it in then they will know we are here and we might lose are only chance at catching Frost. We will call it in as soon as we get done."

I can tell he doesn't agree with this completely. He knows that I am right though. So, he puts down his radio and pulls out his firearm. I do the exact same thing that Smith does. We begin to walk up to the house where Frost supposedly is at the moment.

In most situations we would knock on the door. That would just give Frost time to leave somehow. He does not deserve to have that warning. I want to take him by complete surprise. I want to be able to see the shock in his face when we kick open the door.

I stand back and on the count of three I kick open the front door of Frosts' house. Smith storms in first and I follow directly behind him. Smith goes to the room to the right and I go to the left.

"Clear," I hear Smith say.

I constantly hear him saying that until there is no more

rooms to clear. Smith and I meet up in front of the door.

"Looks like he is not here," Smith said.

At that moment I hear a gun shot go off and watch as detective Smith's body drop to the floor. I hear someone moving upstairs and I dart up behind the the killer. My first thought is that Frost did this. That all goes away when I catch the person in the main bedroom. When I flip over the man it is Smith's CI.

I start to punch him over and over again. I finally stop because I realize that I am killing him. When I stop there is blood coming from his lip. The CI smiles with his bloody teeth.

"Why are you smiling?" I declare.

He points his finger at me and starts to curl it over and over again. As if he is telling me to come in closer. Not thinking I do just that. I put my ear close to his lips.

"Look behind you," he whispers.

I quickly turn around and there is Frost. He takes the butt of a shotgun and drives it straight into my face. I fall back to the floor beside Smith's CI and my vision starts to blur until the point where I completely blackout.

~Chapter 5~

I OPEN MY EYES to an environment that I am not familiar with at all. I have to cover my eyes from the sun blaring straight on me. The sun hurts so bad since I have barely seen it the last couple weeks considering the city of Chicago has been under constant snowfall. Where I am though now is the completely opposite of Chicago.

I stand up to my feet and notice that my shoes that I had on before Frost hit me in the head are gone. I have nothing but my bare feet. I feel my toes in curling in the sand. That is not the only thing though. Frost had taken my shirt as well. The only piece of clothing I had on was my boxers and pants. He even took my belt.

I wonder if this is where he brings his victims and tortures them here. Or worse is this where he kills them. The sad part of this all is that I know exactly where I am. I am on this private island owned by Frost. I know this because we happened to come across it when we were looking for him. If this is the place where he brings his victims then how did he continue to get back and forth? We have had the island on lock down since we found out about it. Shutting off anyway for him to get here. So, how am I here without rescue?

I look down at my pale skin that is not made for this. I

have an Irish background and that is where the reddish tint in my hair comes from. As you probably know most red head humans are paler than most other humans. When they are exposed to much sunlight they tend to burn a whole lot easier.

When I look down at my pale white chest I notice something duck-taped to my stomach. I don't know how I didn't notice it before now that I realized it was there. My stomach and chest have hair on it so this is going to hurt to find out what is behind that duck-taped.
"One...breathe... two... breathe deeper... three..." I say within my mind.
On the count of three I rip the grey tape off my stomach and let out a loud screaming noise. "Shit!" I yell to myself. I don't know why I would let it out it's not like anyone is going to hear me. I am sure that I am alone on this island. A worse thought though just happens to cross my mind. What if Frost has this island as a hunting ground? His prey happens to be his victims. It would not be the first time that something like that would happen.
When I get the tape completely off my body there is something taped to the other side. It is a hand held tape recorder. I quickly open it up to see if there is anything inside. When I do I am lucky (well maybe not so lucky depending on what the recorder says). There is a tape already placed inside the recorder. I immediately hit the play button and the voice that comes on the other side of the tape is all to familiar. At least one thing is familiar today. It is the voice of Scott Frost.
"Hello, detective Gibbs," he starts to say. After a brief pause the voice begins to talk again, "I am Scott Frost, but I am sure you already knew that didn't you? You might think you know where you are but you really don't."
"At least that is what you think," I state to myself.
"You think you are on the island that you and your dead detective friend found in your research. Well you are not. I would tell you where you are but that would be no fun at all. Instead I would rather play a game. The game is simple you have to do five challenges. If you complete all of these task

that are asked of you then you will be rewarded. Your reward will be getting off this island. In addition I will through in a bonus prize. That being said you will get a chance to be face to face with me."

I don't want to play his stupid ass games because that just means I will be doing what he wants. Though being able to meet Frost face to face and complete my revenge would be a cherry on the top for me. So instead of stopping the tape right then and there I continue to listen.

"If you are still listening then your first task is simple like I said before. I know that you can not swim, but if you want to get one step closer to a face to face with your wife's killer then you will learn quickly. About fifty yards out into the ocean there is a bottle tied to a boulder at the bottom of the ocean. Your task is to go and get the bottle. If you get this bottle successfully then you will only have four more challenges. I hope to hear from you soon detective Gibbs."

~Chapter 6~

THE TAPE RECORDER stops playing Frosts' voice. I play the tape one more time just to see if I can find any clues at all as to what Frost has planned for me. I find nothing though. All I get out of the tape is that if I do Frosts' stupid task that I will see him in person and finally get my revenge.

I still don't know if me doing the test are the best move on my part though. I just feel that if I do them that I will be letting Frost win at his own game. After all he does have the advantage, he has me on a second island that I don't know about. He is in control of all the games in some way I am sure of it. The crazy thing about all of this is that ,I thought Smith and I had dug up a lot of information on Frost. But I was wrong because compared to the information that Frost has on me I have nothing on him. He knows everything about me. He knew where I lived and murdered my wife. Now he revealed to me that he knows even little personal information that only my wife and some of my close friends knew. How does he find out information like that. It is not in my report that I don't know how to swim. That is just private information.

I try for a third and final time to listen to the tape. Once again I am left with no answer as to any clues as to Frosts' plan. I put the tape recorder in the sand. I strip down to my boxers and place my pants right beside the recorder. It is pretty sad I had everything just two months ago and now all I have is my boxers, my pants, a tape recorder, and a heart full of revenge.

    I walk very slowly towards the huge body of water. Between the nervous pit in my stomach and my knees shaking tremendously I don't know which is slowing me down more. I take another step and my right foot is now in the water. The water is so cold and feels amazing right now considering how hot it is.

    I take step after step until the water is at neck level. I am debating internally if I should go in the rest of the way or not. Like it was said before I am not a good swimmer. Now the waves are starting to roll in over my head and I feel my feet barely being able to touch the bank any longer. I stand on my tip-toes till they will no longer touch either. I take one last deep breathe and start to doggy paddle. It is a sorry excuse for a doggy paddle, but it is one in any event.

    I am about thirty yards out when I began to doggy paddle. And I have been doing that for about ten yards. So I only have about ten more yards to go when I decide to go under water. I dive deeper and deeper towards the bottom of the sea. I am a smoker and a drinker so it is hard to hold my breathe for a longer period of time.

    I feel the water starting to sip into my mouth and feeling my lungs. I start to ascend back up towards the sun so that I can breathe healthy oxygen again. After getting my breathe once more I dive back down and look around. I am about ready to give up and go back to the surface when I see a glare out of the corner of my eye. I quickly dive to the object with barely any room left in my lungs. I reach the object and just as Frosts message said the bottle is tied to a boulder. I start to try to untie the bottle, but can't at first. I rise to the surface once more. When I go back down I know where the bottle is. So, I don't have to waste my breathe on searching anymore. I can use all my oxygen towards untying that damn rope. I take a big breathe. A bigger one than I did the other two times I descended.

    I reach the bottle and start to work on it again. Finally minutes later the bottle breaks free of the rope. I grab the rope and head back up-top. This time though I go at an angle back towards the island rather than straight up to the surface. I think I am starting to get the hang of this swimming thing. Well, I should have paid attention to my surroundings instead of being overwhelmed with joy because I passed the first task.

    That simple mistake caused me to not think straight. I have been under water for about five minutes now. Since I took the angle rather than a straight path towards the surface I am no where close to fresh air. I fill my body filling of water and as the oxygen runs out of my body I begin to faint. For the second time in less than twenty four hours my eyes close and I pass out.

~*Chapter 7*~

I OPEN MY EYES to that damn bright sun again. Don't get me wrong I enjoy seeing the sun considering I didn't get to see you that much back in Chicago. But it is so damn bright.

"Wait... How am I here on this island again?" I say internally.

Last thing I remember was passing out in the middle of the ocean. Usually that would result in me drowning. Actually that would be the same result in most cases not just mine. So once again I question, how am I here again? Maybe the waves pushed me inland (I was not that far out. That could be a possibility.). Or maybe it was something entirely different (Like Frost.). If he wanted me to die he would have killed me back in Chicago. So, the bigger question is what is his end game?

I let this question bother me for a few dozen moments before I remembered the bottle. I look to my side and right there it is. It must have been Frost who saved me. There is no way that bottle magically landed in the same spot I did. None of that matters right now. My attention is completely drawn to the bottle because I notice that something is in it that was not when I first got it from the oceans floor.

I can not make out what it is at all. I look around to find something to break the bottle. Should be a simple task and it would be if the bottle was glass. The bottle just so happened to be a plastic water bottle. I start digging in the sand and try to find something, or anything.

I feel my fingers smash into something rough. I grab it and pull it from the sand. It is a small rock and lucky for me it just happens to have a sharp edge to it. I take the sharp corner of the rock and start cutting into the plastic bottle. I try to do it carefully because I am not sure what is inside.

Finally the plastic bottle is completely opened and I quickly grab the object from inside. It is another tape for my recorder.

"Oh shit the recorder," I yell as I stand up.

I calm down immediately though because right near I woke up is my pants and the recorder. I sigh a breathe of relief. I run over to the spot. I scurry to put on my pants and then I pick up the recorder. I go to eject the first tape that I listen to before, but it is no longer there.

I try to ignore this unusual clue. I don't think it is a clue to myself, but it is. I place the second tape inside the recorder.

"Hello, again detective Gibbs," Frost says over the recorder.

I really hate his voice. I am not annoyed with it or just tired of it. I just absolutely hate the sound that comes out of his mouth.

"Congratulations you passed the first task. Well sort of in a way. I knew that you would not make it back to the island. When I knocked you out the first time I poisoned you. When you fainted in the ocean I picked you and your task up. I also arranged for the preparation of task number two," Frost says.

I drop to my knees before listening to the rest of the tape. The pain that shoots through my head is incredible. My vision gets blurred and I expect that I am about to pass out again. This time though instead of seeing darkness I see a flash of light. The light travels through a tunnel and at the end of a tunnel I see something. I notice what it is now. It is a vision, but it doesn't make any sense at all.

I see a young boy in a bath tub playing with a little rubber duck. A woman is bathing him when a man walks in. The woman looks scared to death as the man approaches them.

"Back away," she says.

The man slaps the woman and then he approaches the little boy. He takes the little boys head and shoves it into the bath water, drowning him. Seconds later the woman hits the man with the back of the toilet.

"Now get out of my house!!" She yells.

The vision fades away and I snap back into reality.

"What in the hell was that?" I say aloud.

I start to reply the recorder again.

"The second task is just as simple as the first. For you though it is even easier, since you like to hunt. And I promise no poison this time. You have my word. Now lets get past that corny moment. Your second task is to find an animal on the island that is tattooed with a target on the side of it. Keep your eye out for this animal could be anywhere and can easily slip by you. There is a pocket knife in your pants pocket. Remember after this task you will only have three more. Look forward to seeing you soon detective."

~Chapter 8~

    I HIT THE STOP button on the side of the recorder. I want to slam the damn thing onto the ground and shatter it into a million little tiny pieces. But I can't because I need it, unfortunately. I just slid it back into my pocket. I don't waste my time trying to listen to the tape again because I know Frost is not leaving clues anymore. He is going straight to the point. I must follow his game in order to do what I need to do.

    The sun is beginning to fall. I must find shelter because without knowing where I am I can not know how night will effect my process.

    I take the knife that I found thanks to Frost and begin building me a shelter from the material around me. It should be hard work for me to do this. At first it is because I started to cut on a tree. It doesn't take long that like usual I am wasting my time. From behind a bush I see a stock pile of the material I need to build my shelter. Must be Frost who did it. It is almost as if Frost wants me to find him. I know that sounds crazy, but he is laying everything out for me perfectly so that he leads me straight to him. He must know what I will do if I meet up with him face to face. I know it is a little crazy, but I plan on killing him when I find him.

I begin to put the pieces together of wood. Finally I finish and my hut is complete. The only thing I have left is to find food and start a fire to cook it.

I build a pile from the remaining wood. Following that, I start the fire and let it build up as I go out to hunt. The first thing that I find I must eat because I don't know how much animal life is here on the island. So, I must not drag my hunt on. I need to find it fast for another reason though.

I look up at the clouds and the brightness that filled the sky just hours before is now covered in dark scary looking clouds. I must get back before the storm hits so that I can have some kind of shelter. That and I need to cook my food first. I don't worry to much about the things that trouble my mind though because I am sure that Frost has arranged for me to find food. After all he did say that there was animals here. I guess I just need to find the right one. But that is for tomorrows task. Today is just finding me dinner, and if everything fails I am sure I can catch a fish from the ocean.

I start my way inland to find my food. It does not take me very long before I stubble across something. I hear the rattling of the grass and leaves coming from behind a bush. I quickly dropped down so that whatever it is doesn't see me.

I don't know if it is something as big as a deer, or as small as a rat. Soon enough though I will be eating it. I creep closer towards the noise. One small step at a time until I am directly in front of it. I am just on the other side of the bush.

"Three...two...one..." I say internally. It's not like I could say it out loud because then it would scare away the prey. On one I jump over the bush with fiery look on my face and knife in my hand.

As I reach the other side of the bush there is black bunny laying there eating some grass. The poor rabbit had no chance at all. Before it noticed I was coming it was already under the blade of my knife. I watch as the blood pours out of the dead animal. A perfect meal, neither to big or to small. I turn around to the bush and clean my blade from the rabbit's blood. When I turn back around I notice something wrong with my trophy. It is moving around, but that is not possible because I am certain that it is dead.

Well it looks like cleaning my blade was for nothing. I stab the poor animal again to put him out of his misery. Well maybe it is a she I really am not sure. When I stab the rabbit this time my blade has more blood on it than it did the first time. I move the rabbit's body and underneath lays a dead little mouse.

My first thought is what luck I must be having. This can be my snack for the night. I pick the mouse up by its tail along with the rabbit in my other hand. I immediately drop the rabbit though as soon as I take a good look at the other side of the mouse.

I see a darken target symbol tattooed on the side of the mouse. I was not expecting this to be this easy. I had not even been looking for the animal and found it. It must be fate me being on this island. It must be fate to come face to face with Frost.

That is the last thing I think at the moment because that tunnel of light is back and with it another vision. This time it is another vision, but it is the same bathroom as the old vision. The young boy though this time is at the sink or so I suppose it is the little boy again. All I can see is the hands of what appears to be a young child's.

The pair of hands are holding two things over the sink. In one hand is a knife and in the second hand is a little brown mouse. The sink in the beginning of the vision was a pearly white, but that is not the case now. The once white sink is now got a dripping red liquid pouring into it. The blood is coming from the mouses neck where the knife had just sliced it.

I snap back into reality and I am so confused as to what the hell is going on. I don't understand why I am having these visions. More importantly though who are the people in the vision?

I successfully get back to the camp site before the rain begins to fall. I put the rabbit on the fire to cook and I bring the mouse to the sheltered area.

I quickly placed the new tape inside the recorder where

the old one was.

"Detective, you are one step close to finding me. I would congratulate you, but these tasks have been so simple up to now. Your final three missions will have more of a challenge I am sure. Enough about that for a moment. I bet you are wondering what those visions are all about. Well you know when the detective catches the serial killer one of the questions that are always asked what is going through there mind. Well if you ever catch me you can tell the world my side of the story. How did I become who I am today? You will be able to tell my memories to the world," he states.

That son-of-a-bitch has effected my mind.

"I know it is a lot to sink it at the moment. So I will give you a minute."

Well he lied that minute was more like a millisecond.

"Hahaha. I am just kidding I have no heart. Your next task is in the exact middle of the island. You will not be able to miss it. There will be a bunker with a message on the front door. There is someone in there that I know you are dying to meet. I will talk to you soon Gibbs."

The recorder shuts off and the rain begins to down pour.

~*Chapter 9*~

I OPEN MY EYES after a decent nights sleep. If I am telling the truth I did not sleep very well at all. The thunder and lightening kept me up most of the night. That was not what kept me up the other part though. When the stormed passed I kept hearing the cracking of twigs and the movement of disturbing leaves.

Like I have said many times before I don't know what is all on this island. Knowing Frost he has brought all kinds of weird species to this environment. He is after all a weird species himself.
Then again the noises I keep hearing could just be Frost. Or the person from the bunker is escaping. The more likely story though is Frost of those two.

I rub my eyes until they are almost raw I am sure of it. Finally I get my vision all the way back. I walk out of the shelter area and have to close my eyes right back because I am blinded by the sun. I still am not use to the sun being so bright. I walk to the shore and to the edge of the water.

I take my hands and pick up a hand full of sea water. I splash it on my face and oh how I wish I didn't. The cut where Frost hit me yesterday morning with the gun is still open. Once that water hits my wound I immediately grab it. The burning sensation is incredible. I try to dig the burning feeling out, but it only gets worse.

Finally after the time that I lost count on the pain goes away. I will definitely not make that same mistake again. I make sure everything is in place the way it should be and then I head in the direction of the middle of the island.

I hear the birds chirping and still the movement of everything around me. I am starting to feel that someone is following me. But I am sure that is just my vivid imagination.

It is about twelve o'clock in the afternoon when I notice a big bush in the middle of everything. This is no ordinary bush. It is almost as if the bush is hiding something behind it. I walk straight up to it and move part of the bush back. When I do right there the bunker door is.

Just as he said before there is a message on the door. The message looks to be written in blood. I wouldn't be surprised with Frosts' misguided mind.

Your next tapes are located inside the object.

What is that suppose to mean? The only thing I know for sure that is in this bunker is someone that I am dying to apparently meet.

I open the bunker door and walk in. I move around looking for a light to give some vision to this room. Finally I find it and when I do there is a long hallway with doorways to either side.

It would take me forever to find which room this mysterious person was in if it wasn't for my path. The blood that was on the door continues on with several arrows that lead to the very last door on the right. When I reach this door I walk in. When I do a light immediately comes on. When it does a man is located in the middle of the room. He is taped and chained to a chair just as the recorder was taped to my stomach yesterday.

Frost said I would like to meet this person, but I have no idea who it is. I wish those two things where the thing that I noticed the most. On the both of the mans forearm I see his skin raised up in a perfect rectangle shape.

"Holy shit," I exclaim.

The mans eyes where closed until I opened my mouth. I should have kept my mouth shut , but I know now what the message meant on the door. Frost has put the tapes inside the mans forearms. What kind of sick and twisted game is this one?

I can tell how he put one of the tapes in the mans arm. He just simply cut and stitch back the skin over top of the tape. The other one though there is no cut marks or anything I honestly have no clue how he did it. The more important answer though is how do I get that one out?

I take my knife over to the man and cut the first tape out of his arm. I wipe the tape off and then place it in the recorder as I have so many times before now.

"Detective Gibbs you must be wondering what is going on. Well like I said I have placed a man before you that I know you have been dying to meet. This mans name is Richard Carr. Does it still not ring a bell. Well, let me put it in black and white for you. This man before you is your father."

A very disgusted look comes over my faces. I had not seen my father since I was a little boy. Not since before my mother passed away.

"This man is who left you and your mother alone. I know you personally have been looking for him for years for another purpose. They said the fire that was set that killed your mother was done by the hands of this man. I now give you the chance to get your revenge on him for killing her. You have two choices here detective. You either kill this man and take the other tape from his arm the same way he took your mothers life. Or you can get the tape out and let the man live. The choice is yours," the recorder says.

~Chapter 10~

I SHUT THE recorder off as I stare at the man that is my father. Frost was right about one thing. I had been looking for Mr. Carr since I came into the police force. So that I could look into the eyes of the man that killed my mother.

I go over to Carr and grab him by what hair he has left. I stare into the mans eyes. It is a tactic that I like to do back at the station because I try to see what they seen in their eyes. I usually see nothing but a dark soulless pit in them.

In my father though I don't see the same dark eyes that I have seen in the other convicted killers that I have put behind bars. Instead I see just the mans green eyes.

I rip the tape off of Carr's mouth.

"Did you kill my mother?"

The man takes a minute to gather everything and then says, "No. I loved your mother."

I slap the poor excuse for a man as soon as the last words roll off his tongue.

"If you loved her then why did you leave? And watch what you say because I can easily slap you again."

"Your mother left me and when I came back to try to fix things you guys had already moved."

I continue to stare into his eyes. There is no lie in those eyes either. I turn around to catch my breathe so that I can absorb everything I just heard. When I do I see a torch in the corner. It is already plugged into the wall and everything for me.

I go over and grab the torch and start towards Carr. His eyes are full of fear now as I approach him.

"I am sorry I am doing what I must," I tell him.

I don't give the man a chance to respond before I start to burn his flesh. The smell is not describable, it is just absolutely terrible. That is not the only sense that is hurting. I should have put the tape back over his mouth before doing this. He is screaming like a little girl. I don't blame him though because I would probably be doing the exact same thing.

I finally finish and grab the second tape from his forearm. I then think about what to do next. I take the knife that I used many times now and head back towards my father. I can tell he is preparing for me to kill him. I instead cut him lose from the chair.

"Thank you," he says.

"Don't thank me. Now get the hell out of here."

"No. I don't know where I am. We should stick together," he tries to explain.

"There is no we in this. I want nothing you have. You didn't help me before and your not helping me now."

"I do have something you want," Carr says.

"Oh and what might that be?" I question.

"Promise me if I tell you that you will let me stick around."

"Yeah okay."

"I know the real person who started that fire that killed your mother."

I look up at his eyes once more and again the man tells no lies.

~Chapter 11~

I REACH OUT MY hand and shake his hand in agreement.
"You have a deal," I state to him.
"Maybe I should kill him after all," I hear someone say.
"What did you say?" I snare back at Carr.
"Nothing," he declares.
I shake my head to clear it. I then grab the second tape and place it in the recorder. Then that dreadful voice hits my ears again.
"If you are listening to this tape I am sure that you let your father live. After all that is what I come to expect from you. You have a reputation for letting murders go. First you took your time catching me and you see what happened to your wife. I wonder what will happen since you let your father live. No matter all of that though. We have business to discuss now don't we? For your fourth task it is probably the easiest task of all. Those voices that you are hearing. All you have to do is let them in."

How in the hell does he know I have heard strange voices? I have been hearing them ever since I been on the island. Maybe it is a side effect of that drug he gave me. Just like the visions he planted into my head. Just another part of his game.

"Now of course I will not know if you truly let the voices in or not. So, this task will be a matter of trust."

There is no way in hell that I am letting those voices in. I don't want to cheat my wife though. So maybe I must because he could really have a way to know or not. Even though he says he doesn't. I am not sure how to do this at all.

"I let the voices in," I say internally to them.

"Congratulations Gibbs you just earned your ticket to the final task. Well hear it is. Your final task is what you have been waiting on for since you got on the island. You just have to find me and like all the other task this one will be simple as well. Across the hall from this room is a door. Just enter it and there I will be. I look forward to seeing you very soon detective Gibbs."

The recorder shuts off for the final time. I no longer need it and when I no longer need something I ditch it. I go over to the torch that I just used moments before on my father. I pick it up and light that damn recorder on fire.

"Son," I hear as I feel a touch on my shoulder from Carr.

"Don't call me that!" I exclaim.

"I don't know what kind of game this guy is trying to play with you, but you need to ignore him."

"I don't need your advice. You lost that ability a long time ago."

I storm out the door and head right across the hall just like Frost says.

"Stay out here. This is between Frost and I."

My father nods his head even though he doesn't agree. I walk right into the room and close the door behind me.

"Welcome detective Gibbs," Frost says from the shadows.

He steps forward into the light. When he does I am shocked with the way the man looks. I expect him to look creepy or even evil. He looks just like a normal person though. He looks about the age of sixty. Which tells me he has been doing this work for longer than what we thought.

"I am sure I don't need to introduce myself," he says.

"No you don't," I say rudely.

"Well, then lets get to this then. I will not fight you. All of your challenges have been easy up to this point and this will be no different," Frost announces.

He walks over to the corner from where he was at when I first entered the room. He grabs a huge sword and holds it out for me to grab. I slowly reach out and grab the sword because I am confused. Frost then drops to his knees and bends down his head.

It is as if he wants me to kill him. I wait for a second after pulling the sword out of its' cover.

"Oh come on, do it. I didn't waste any time when I murdered your wife."

The blood of rage shoots up to my mind and without any remorse I raise the blade. I proceed to with a firm and quick strike pierce Frosts' neck. I watch as his head rolls off his neck. I drop the the blade to the ground and moments later Carr enters the room.

"Are you okay?" he asks.

"Yeah. Lets get out of here."

Before I can exit the room I notice something in Frosts' hand. I bend down to see what it is. It is another recorder just like mine. I grab the recorder from his dead hands and then stand back up tall. Carr looks at me and I look at him.

"Detective Gibbs congratulations you have completed your revenge. If it was not for me being dead at this moment I would be happy for you. You think my work will end though with my death. It will not for this is just the beginning. I did as I promised you received your revenge and now for the second part of the deal your escape. On the far end of the island there is a boat. It is full of gas and everything. It is about a days travel to the nearest country, Japan. There will be a woman there, my daughter who will help you find your way back to Chicago. Once again congratulations detective and happy hunting," he ends the tape by letting out a evil laugh straight from hell.

"Come on. When we get back home I expect you to keep up your end of the deal," I say to Carr.

"Absolutely."

~Chapter 12~

A COUPLE WEEKS LATER....
I WALK INTO MY new apartment. After my wife's death I quickly sold the house we use to live in. I couldn't stand the fact of living there no more. My Realtor had some kind of deal that if she didn't sell my house within thirty days that her company would buy itself.

Jane Myers is her name. I was for sure that she would be able to sell it from the first meeting we had. There was just something about her. She was so full of confidence that it seemed impossible that she didn't sell it in time. She kept her word about everything though. When the thirty first day came that my house was on the market I got a call.

We had listed the house for two-hundred thousand. This was a very cheap price for the house. I know we could have gotten a whole lot more out of it, but I was in a hurry to get that house in the rear view mirror. When I got the call from Jane I was completely hit with shock. Jane's company knew my story of the reason for getting the house out of the way. They made an offer three-hundred and fifty thousand.

I was very pleased with this offer. Then again who wouldn't be? The money I got from the house plus the money

I plan on getting from my wife's business. I know I should probably keep the company and not spit in the image of her reputation. I just don't have the time or the patience to deal with it all.It really kind of saddens me that I have to sell it. I learn from an early age though life is not always fair.

    I close the door as I walk into the hallway. All of the lights are out in the house except one, the kitchen. I know for a fact though that I turned it off when I left this morning. I lay down my jacket and grab my pistol out of its' holder. I hear clashing of pans coming from the room. Now I know for a fact that someone is in my home.

    I move slowly closer to the light where the noise is coming from. I reach the corner by the kitchen and jump around the corner with my gun held high.

    "Put your hands up in the air," I yell.

    I see someone jump up from the area behind the island counter. This person drops the pans that they have in there hands causing for a loud banging noise to echo throughout my apartment. Seconds later I lower my gun because I realize who it is is. It is Sarah my daughter.

    "I am sorry," she exclaims.

    "It is okay I am just still spooked about everything," I say as I put the gun on the counter.

    "You need to make sure you start calling when you decide to come," I continue on.

    "I did try to call. You never picked up the phone, it went straight to voice mail."

    "Oh yeah. I probably just forgot to pay the bill. What are you even doing here?" I try to answer without being rude.

    "Well, I heard a rumor about you that you're about to sell moms company," she states.

    I don't have to give her an answer because my facial expression tells her the answer she needed to know.

    "You don't have to anymore though. Miss Sarah Gibbs is here to help."

    "What about Stanford?" I declare right away.

    "I can wait on school. Besides me taking over a company like moms I don't need to go to school," she tries to explain.

    Once again I don't give her an answer. This time though

a frustrated look comes upon my face. I finally pick up the courage to say a positive input.

"If you can find a legal way to do it then you have my support."

That saves one problem on my plate. I know I seem mad about it, but the truth is I am happy. As I said before, I felt bad about having to sell her company and with this new terms of events I don't have to sell it.

"Oh and until I get the first couple of months worth of my checks I am going have to move back in with you," she states with a smirk.

My face changes quickly back to frustrated.

"I just got her out of the house," I laugh internally to myself.

One problems fixed the next one begins.

"Okay, baby girl," I reply instead to her with a fake smile.

~*Chapter 13*~

I STEP NERVOUSLY through the doors that read CPD. Normally, I would step through the door with a swagger on my shoulder because I use to feel untouchable. The last time though I walked through this door was the last before I was kidnapped.

Just like that day I have to make a hopeful quick stop at the captains office. I don't know why he is even wanting to see me because he is going to ask the same questions about me being okay to return. Then he will get the same response that he got last time as well.

I walk over to the elevator and hit the up button. I wait patiently for the elevator to come down. A geekish looking man approaches beside me. I recognize him right away. His name is Dustin Jones, and he is the chief medical examiner for the Chicago Police Department. He has been here just as long as I have. Well, that is not the truth. He has been here five months less than I have, but still pretty damn close. Mr. Jones gives me a strange look as we sit there and wait for the elevator.

A ding sound goes off as the doors to the elevator shaft open. Mr. Jones and I step into the little space together. I offer my hand out to him so that he can push his level first. He is going to the basement and we are only one floor away from that. So, why would I go to my floor first when I have two levels to go.

We ride down to the basement, and a jerking motion tugs us from side to side when the elevator comes to a stop at the basement level. The elevator doors open and Mr. Jones walks out.

"I'll see you around, Gibbs," he states.

"I am sure you will, Mr. Jones."

He turns his head around sharply with a death stare. I just smile as the doors close once again. The medical examiner hates being called Mr. Jones because it makes him feel old. Simply things like that just make me get through the day. The elevator goes on to the third floor and comes to stop once again. The ding noise repeats itself as the door opens for the last time.

I step out and expect to see Tara at the desk, but she is not. That just means she is in the captains office then again. The ding from the elevator though is loud enough so that they can be alarmed for incoming people. I just sit out in the lobby for Tara to come out. When she does she is buttoning up her shirt and adjusting her double d size bra.

"The captain is ready for you," she states.

"I bet he is," I mumble to myself under my breathe.

I then proceed into the captains office. He is adjusting his pants and sit down in his seat.

"Hey, James. Come on in and sit down. You doing alright?"

"First off so we don't have repeat moment of last time I was up here, I am perfectly fine. I just want to get back to work."

The captain shakes his head in agreement.

"Well, I will get straight to the reason I called you up here. Next week you have a court date to explain the events that happened on the island. We already have a lawyer and everything set up for you. The lawyer says if you say if it was self-defense you should be fine."

"Should be?" I snare.

"You did kill someone, James. Even if the man was a no good son-of-a-bitch. Your lucky they haven't picked you up yet. I also was able to overturn the ruling of suspending you until then.

"What?" I yell.

"You went against what I told you about not going after Frost. Plus it is usually protocol for you to be suspended when under a criminal investigation. So really you should be thanking me for saving your ass," he declares.

I think about what he said before I respond. He is right though he could have threw me under the bus, but instead he stood up for me. That is what a true partner does though. That is why I will never have another partner like him.

"Thank you," I respond.

"Now, get down stairs and go meet your new partner."

"Yes, sir."

I go to leave, but before I can I am stopped by the captain saying the last word, "And James if you pull some bullshit with this new partner like you did the old one I will fire you," He states angrily.

I say nothing and walk out the door to meet my new partner.

~*Chapter 14*~

I DECIDE TO TAKE the stairway on the way back down to the second floor. I think it would be pointless for me to take an elevator for just one floor. I will probably get downstairs before the elevator ever reaches where I wait at. Then again I did take it for just two floors. So, don't ask or judge me. I have a lot of shit going on right now.

I reach my desk and look around for any new faces to see if I can find out who my new mystery partner is. I still think it is a little strange that the captain never gave me a name. Oh well I am sure I will find out soon enough. Still though I wish who I knew it was now so I can get the bullshit introduction over with.

I continue to look around, but I see no new face. There is something out of place though I notice as a woman is walking towards me. The woman that is walking towards me I know. I know her very well actually. I had known her since she had been in diapers so this face is all to familiar to me. This woman's name is Jenni Green, the captains' daughter.

I know this can not be so. I don't believe she was even old enough to go to threw police academy. Or maybe she was

I have been flustered minded lately. I try to think hard about her age. Finally it pops into my head. She did turn twenty-one at the beginning of this year. Still why would captain partner me up with his daughter? It doesn't make sense at all to me.

Then she reaches my desks and stops right on the spot.

"Hey, James," she says with her red lips.

Looking at Jenni and not talking to her you definitely would not guess that she was becoming a cop. She has long blonde curly hair, and brown eyes. She honestly looks like ones of those girls that you see in the magazines that model.

I ask her the first question that pops into my mind without thinking about it, "Do I even need to ask how you were able to by pass officer and go straight to detective?"

"You probably already know the answer," she laughs.

I more than likely do and that answer goes by the name of the captain. I guess that is just a perk of having a father being the leader of the firm.

The only thing that worries me is the talk that is going to go around the office about how she is not qualified. As I said before though she is like a second daughter to me and everyone knows it so they better keep their damn mouth shut around me. And considering its the bosses daughter they better keep it shut or they might lose their job. Or worse their head.

I stand up and hug Jenni like I haven't seen her in ages. She wraps her arms back around me. Usually I would shake my new partners hand and tell them welcome to the team. Jenni though is different. I already knew her before and besides she basically been part of this team for as long she been born with her two fathers being cops.

"So, how have you been?" I ask her.

"Can't complain," she states.

"Well, Sarah is staying in town permanently now. You girls should met and catch up. She is always asking about you," I tell her.

"Sounds good."

Just about then a phone begins to ring at the desk next to mine. Jenni walks over to the desk and answers the phone.

That still going to take some time to getting use to. Who am I to judge though she seems to be doing what she wants to do. Even if someone told her not to or even worse, she couldn't, then there would be hell to pay. She would do the task and then rub it in your face that she actually did it. That is just the kind of girl she is.

Jenni hangs up the phone and finishes writing on the paper that she is caring to.

"So, what do we got?"

"Two bodies were just found at the Soldier Field."

"Let me grab my coat and then we will go," I answer.

I stand to my feet and we leave the station together.

~Chapter 15~

I PULL INTO the unusual empty parking lot. Every time I normally pull into this parking lot it is full of cars, grills, coolers, and of course the crazy fans. Even throughout the week in-season they are filled. I have only been to about fifty games total in my life. The police department gives out tickets every year, and since I have been there past ten years I get tickets to two games a year. That doesn't take into count the amount of tickets I bought out of pocket.

I have been a huge Bears fan since back in the seventies. Like I said before though, this parking lot is usual completely full. On this Saturday before the NFC Championship game this lot is on filled with some cop cars, and the stadium is surrounded by the yellow tape of the crime scene.

I park right next to one of the lines of tapes. Jenni and I get out of the car and walk towards the first layer of security. The dark tall looking man raises the tape for us.

"Where are they at?" Jenni asks the man.

"They are out on the field," he answers as he lowers his head.

"What is it?" I question him because I can tell something is seriously wrong.

The security guard raise his head, and his lips begin to

move, "I have seen a bunch of murder scenes before since I have moved to Chicago. I even have gotten a call to secure the crime scenes of a lot of gang murders."

"Get to the point!" Jenni exclaims.

"This is the worst crime scene I have ever witnessed."

I lay my hand on his shoulder and tell him its going to be okay. From what the guard said I will have to be the judge of all of that. I too have seen a lot of murder scenes that have been terrible. My first though, is still to the date the worse I have ever been part of. My partner at the time had told me that it wasn't going to be that bad and that I just need to let my mind wonder so that I didn't get to emotional over my first dead body. He said that before we found Scott Frosts' first victim.

We then walk throughout the stadium and into the tunnel leading to the field. When we do, I found a new worse murder scene ever. There are two bodies one in either end zone. They both are tied up to either field goal post. The bodies have been appeared to been cut up in several pieces and then sowed back together. Another thing though that is not really unique to the bodies, but with this crazy scene even the little things are unique. Each of the bodies have what appear to be bullet holes in their forehead.

I walk over to one of the bodies as Jenni walks over to the other end.

"Do we have an ID yet on this body?" I ask as I pull out a notebook.

"See for yourself," the officer says.

The officer moves out of the way and I take a glance at the dead body. I put my pen and notebook away for a minute because there is no need for me to write the victims ID on this piece of paper. I know exactly who this person is. He is a male and goes by the name of Hunter James. Mr. James is the tailback for the Chicago Bears, and tomorrow he is suppose to be taking place in the biggest game of his early career. When I say early I mean early, the outstanding M.V.P. of this season is only in his second year.

I finish up everything that I need to do for the investigation and then meet Jenni at the fifty yard line. For those who don't know football terms the fifty yard line is in the exact middle of the field.

"Well our victim over there is no other than Hunter James," I say to Jenni.

"The tail back?" she declares.

"Yeah," I reply with a strange look.

"What? Can't a girl know her football?" she laughs.

There is a slight pause for a moment.

"Well, what have you found out your victim?"

"I know exactly who she is and I bet you don't."

I glad she can find some kind of challenge out of this moment. That will be a good thing for her to have during her time as a detective.

"Her name is Brittany Johnson."

I raise my eyebrows as to tell her she was right about me not knowing the name.

"She is a Chicago Bulls cheerleader."

Great not only one iconic name, but two.

"That is not it."

"What now?" I answer her.

"The officer said there is a message for you."

"For me!" I exclaim.

"Yeah," she says as she points to the wall behind the goal post behind Brittany's body.

When I look where Brittany is pointing at a deep sickening feeling comes inside my stomach. I don't know how I didn't notice it before. Probably because my eye sight sucks, and I couldn't see that far anyways. The only reason I knew what Brittany's body looked like is because I seen Hunter's body first and they seemed to appear in the same position. Back to that feeling deep down in my stomach.

On the sideline way behind her body written in the blood of probably the victims are these words, *"I told you detective Gibbs that my work would continue."*

I feel sick to my stomach as I read the words. I hang my head and turn around to where I can't see either one of the victims. I can't help but to think did this happen because I killed Frost. And all he is trying to do is prove a point.

~*Chapter 16*~

I PULL OUT MY chair to the desk and place my self in it. My chair is so much more comfortable than anyone else in the station. They have those hard seat ones that if you sit down in it for more than hour you feel like an ninety-five year old man when you get up. I place my feet up on my desk and wait for my partner to approach me from the other side of the room.

She finally stops talking to some of the other cops. She then walks my way. You would think that someone would run out of breathe and quit talking eventually. Not Jenni though. My wife was so quite when she was alive. This generation of women though does not know the meaning of that.

"So, do we have any information about the victims yet? Like what in the world they have in common beside they are involved in the sports world." I ask her as she steps on my desk.

It takes a minute for me to get the entire sentence out because of her. When she sits down in front of me I can't help but to notice her ass. I know it is a bad thing to notice, but I am still a man. It is in my nature to look when you are single. Even sometimes when your not, but I was always faithful to my wife.

I didn't notice that I was staring at it. That is probably the reason I don't notice her answering my question. Seconds later I see her waving her hand in front of my face to break my concentration. I snap back into reality.

"What did you say?" I say.

"James Gibbs were you just staring at my ass?" she blurts out.

My face turns red because everyone on this floor is staring at me. She didn't say it quite it at all. She just says it out loud.

"W-e-e-e-ll, no I was looking at," I pause to come up with an excuse. Then it hits me and I immediately answer with, "That piece of paper behind you."

The room all turns their attention back to what they were doing before the interruption. I probably shouldn't have looked at it. It was wrong of me. She is my best friends daughter and I am double her age.

"What were you saying about the case?" I ask her as I try to change the subject.

"I was saying no. We have not found out anything at all. The only thing that we can see they have in common is like you said, sports," she answers.

"Something will come up I am sure of it. It always does," I reply.

Not always at least. I was just trying to tell her that because I wanted to keep up her confidence. She stands up and starts walking away.

"Where are you going?" I yell like an angry parent.

"Someone needs to let the families know before they find out over the news," Jenni says.

She does have a point. I stand up and push in my chair. I then follow her to the elevator. When the doors close she pushes the up button on the wall.

"I thought you were leaving the station,"

"We are suppose to go see the captain first,"

"We?" I snare.

"I knew you would come, after all you really were staring at my ass."

My checks turn red again as the elevator doors open. She walks out first and once again my eyes drift down to her ass. I follow her and go to the captains' door. We walk straight in without knocking. Well, there goes my special privilege of being the only one who just walks in the captains office.

When we walk through the door I can tell this is not going to be the pleasant conversation that it usually is. Captain Green has a furious look on his face.

As soon as I shut the door behind me he starts in on us. He doesn't even offer us a chair. Well, it is more like he is starting in on me rather than us.

"Don't you think it would have been a nice bit of information to tell us that Frost planned on having a copycat?" he yells.

The door opens and Tara is standing in its place.

"Is everything okay?" she questions him.

"Yes, now get out," he screams back at her.

She immediately shuts the door behind her and then the captain looks back at me. He must be waiting for an answer I suppose.

"He let me kill him. I figure the tape was just him talking crazy and trying to play mind games even after his death," I try to explain.

"I warned you that if you put my daughter in danger what I would do."

Before he finishes his sentence, Jenni steps in and stands up for me.

"Dad quit. I can look out for myself. I am sure that if you were in the situation that detective Gibbs was in you too would act the same," she declares.

David shuts up for a minute because I am sure he didn't expect her to step in and say something.

"Alright get out of here and go tell the families about their losses," the captain states.

We head out of the room and stop when he starts to speak again, "And detective Green when we are at work it is captain to you."

She responds with no answer and storms out of the door straight to the elevator. When we get in and the doors close to make sure Tara (the captains eyes and ears) can't hear, Jenni starts to mumble the words, "He is such a dick."

I do nothing, but smirk a little.

~Chapter 17~

I LOOK AT THE computer that is in my lap. The address we are looking for reads 356 South Morris Lane.

"That is it," I announce to Jenni as I am pointing over towards a blue house.

The first family we are suppose to be talking to is Miss Johnsons' family. Jenni pulls the car over to the curb by the house. We get out and walk up to the door.

"I will take the lead this time. But next time it is your turn," I declare to Jenni.

She nods her head in agreement as I knock on the door. It takes a minute or two before we hear footsteps approaching the door. Finally, the door opens and a woman's head pokes around it.

The woman looks like a crack head, but who am I to judge?

"Yes? How may I help you?" the woman answers.

"Are you Mrs. Johnson?"

"Yes, who are you?" she snares with a dirty look.

"I am detective Gibbs and this is my partner detective Green. Are you Brittany Johnsons' mother?"

"Yeah. What kind of trouble is she in this time?" she questions again.

"None at all, but we would like to talk to you."

"No offense detectives, but if she is not in any trouble at all then I can't help you. Ever since she got that cheer leading job for the Bulls I lost contact. That was a little over three years ago," Mrs. Johnson states.

Jenni steps forward and takes the reins over.

"Mrs. Johnson. Your daughter was found dead earlier today at Soldier Field."

Even though Mrs. Johnson and Brittany had not been close the last three years you can tell that she is hurt by this. She opens the door while the tears begin to roll down her cheek. She lets us in and she leads us to the living room.

"Have a seat. I will be right back," Mrs. Johnson tells them.

Jenni and I expect for her to go get a tissue for her tears. My detective instincts kick in as I look around the room. Almost every single picture in the house has Brittany in them some how. You can tell that Mrs. Johnson loved her daughter very much. Which would probably be the reason that Mrs. Johnson starting doing her drugs.

I am sure it doesn't take ten minutes for someone to go get a tissue.

"Do you see her anywhere from where you are at?" I question Jenni from the other side of the room. Jenni looks around the corner and shakes her head no.

I am instantly concerned. I nod my head for Jenni to start searching one part of the house while I do the other half. I walk around the house and find nothing. I hear Jenni yell my name from the other part of the house.

I run to where her voice is coming from and stop when I get to her. Mrs. Johnson is on hanging from a rope tied to the top of the shower.

I grab my phone and dial the numbers nine-one-one.

"This is detective Gibbs. I am reporting a suicide."

"Is the victim dead?" the phone says.

I ask Jenni and she confirms Mrs. Johnson death.

"Yes," I answer.

"What is the address?"

"356 South Morris Lane."

"They are on their way," the man on the other side of the phone.

~Chapter 18~

I OPEN MY EYES and sit up in my bed. I reach out my hand and slap the alarm clock on my small dresser beside my bed. The clock reads 7:45 p.m. I decided after a such a long day at work I needed to take a nap before trying to figure out what the two victims have in common.

Jenni and I have been trying to figure it out all day. It has been less than twenty-four hours though. So at least we still have plenty of time. The only bad thing about time is when will the murderer strike next. If he is a prodigy of Frost then I am sure he will make it quick.

I walk out of my bedroom and go to the living room where Sarah is watching television. Nothing important is on at the moment. Just another reality tv show. My daughter's generation have evolved the technology of television so much. It's just these reality shows are so stupid.

"Which show are you watching tonight?" I question her.

"Its' called Naked and Afraid," she responds.

"Do I even ask?"

"Probably not," she laughs.

I walk to the kitchen and go towards the fridge. I grab the gallon of milk and begin to drink from it.

"I seen you on the news earlier," Sarah declares.

I lower the gallon of milk and then question her, "What?"

"Those two murders at the stadium. I seen you entering the field from one of the news video tapings."

"Oh yeah that."

"How did it happen?"

"You know I can't give out information to an investigation," I state. I pause and then continue, "Hey help me clean up a little bit. Jenni Green is coming over to help me with the case."

A shock and pissed off look comes onto Sarahs' face.

"So, you can't tell your own daughter about the investigation but you can tell her. Wow dad okay," she yells.

I just laugh because where Jenni and my daughter have been out of touch for so long she probably has no clue that Jenni is a detective.

"I am really glad you think this is funny. That really just pissed me off."

"Jenni is my new partner at work," I laugh again.

"Oh," Sarah says as her face turns back to normal.

"Now will you help me straighten up a little bit?"

Sarah walks over to me and gives me a kiss on the cheek. "Of course dad."

About that time the door bell rings throughout the apartment. I signal for Sarah to go get the door. She grunts, but does it anyways. Seconds later she returns with Jenni.

Jenni is in a light blue tee shirt and a pair of black yoga pants. I guess I go the wrong impression of what this was going to be. She looks like a sixteen year old girl going to a sleep over.

"Hey James," she says.

"Hey Jenni. Have a seat and I will go get my case file so far," She reaches in her bag and brings out a bag of Chinese food.

"I figure we would eat first. It gives me a chance to catch

up with Sarah," she states.

I really wish that we could just get the work part done first. Then I remember how close my daughter and Jenni use to be. I continue to think of everything my daughter has been through lately.

"That is fine with me. Let me get some plates and glasses," I say with a smile.

~Chapter 19~

I PICK UP EVERYONES plate and take it to the sink to wash. I just listen as Jenni and Sarah laugh about stories of their past. There is one story though that they start to describe that makes me visualize it.

It was ten years ago when Jenni was eleven, and my daughter was ten. We took a trip down to a place in Kentucky name Land Between the Lakes. They call it this because the land that the camp ground is between Kentucky Lake and Barkley Lake.

There was David, Shyanne, Jenni, Sarah, and myself. We went down there for the Fourth of July. The kids swam till they passed out. As for us adults we also passed out, but we were knocked out from alcohol. We usually would just do everything up in Chicago on a typically fourth. It had been five year anniversary of David's wife death. To get the minds off of the unfortunate date for a little bit we planned the trip. Now that my wife is dead I understand why that weekend should have never been planned. I truly get the pain that David felt all those years ago and get that he never had his mind off of his dead wife.

I snap back to my apartment when one of the knives in the sink cut my hand.

"Oh shit," I snare.

"What?" The two girls say in unison.

"Oh nothing. I just cut my hand is all. Nothing serious it is not deep," I say.

"I'm going to go get a band-aid. You need go to the bathroom and wash it up," Sarah says.

I don't even argue with her and just head straight to the bathroom. I begin to rinse it off and one of those visions that I had on the island. The one of the little boys hands cutting the pets neck. I snap back in and out of reality till finally I fall to the floor. Seconds later Jenni and Sarah come to my rescue and help me to my feet.

"Are you sure you want to work tonight? You really could use some rest," Jenni tries to sound concern.

"No I am fine. Just lost a little more blood than what I thought," I try to convince them.

They know there is no point in arguing with me so they don't even try. They walk out of the room and give me a second to recover. When I make a full recovery I walk to the dining room to the table where Jenni is waiting for me. Sarah is back in the living room watching television again.

"You okay now?" I get asked from Jenni as I sit down beside her. After she asks she places her hand on my thigh. I am not sure how to take it at all. I have to hurry and move it though for two reasons. One I am sure is obvious. She is a cute girl and she is touching my inner thigh. Second reason is because Sarah is looking this way. I have to move it immediately, but slowly because Sarah has not noticed it yet.

I finish getting her hand off and she smiles at me. I can't help but to smile back.

"So, anything new on the case?" I try to change the subject.

"No, nothing at all. Mr. James' wife said that he had many enemies. Then again what celebrity doesn't though in this world," Jenni states.

She has a point though. If you're a celebrity it might be all high and mighty, but once you become one you better put a security team on you because you just painted a target on your back.

"And nothing new on Miss Johnson?"

"Nothing."

I frown a terrible face. Just as that happens Sarah walks into the room. She musty have been listening or she wouldn't have came into the room.

"You guys really need to start watching television," Sarah tells us.

"Why?" Jenni asks.

"Because if you guys ever watched TMZ then you would know that both James and Johnson have been hanging out a lot lately. Maybe they have been dating."

"That is absurd. His wife said he was constantly home when he was not at practice," Sarah states.

"Well, no disrespect to Mr. James wife, but she is a damn liar. There is video and pictures of them out in public together." Sarah insists.

She then walks over to the counter and grabs her jacket.

"Where are you going?" I ask her.

"Somewhere," she snares.

She then storms out of the room.

"You really should take it easy on her," Jenni tells me.

"I just want whats best for her is all."

"I know," is all she responds before stopping.

She looks behind me. I then turn around and see what she is staring at. Sarah is standing before us with a piece of paper in her hands. She is standing frozen.

"What is it dear?" I question.

She hands the paper to me. It reads the following, "*I would like to play a game detective Gibbs. Just simply remember is all I ask. My name will be revealed in all good time. Just as Frost was before me. I am his prodigy. And detective Frost murder scenes are nothing compared to what mine will be. There will be more to this game, and there will be blood. I know where you sleep.*
XOXO, Chevy.

I put the paper in my pocket and I grab both of the girls. I hold them in tight to at least protect them for one more night. For as the "Chevy Killer" says there will be blood.

~Chapter 20~

ABOUT A WEEK LATER...

I WALK OVER TO Jenni's desk where she is currently sitting. I get no hello or good morning from her. Instead I get this response, "What in the hell are you doing here?"

"Uh working just like every other Monday morning."

"You are suppose to be at court this morning."

"Oh shit. I completely forgot all about it."

"Come on, I'll drive," she declares.

"No, I need you to run up a lead on that Island I was kidnaped on. It was not in Frosts name and we need to figure out whose name it is in. That might get us one step closer to his accomplish."

"That can wait. Like I said before I am driving."

"And I said no."

We wrestle around for the ownership of the keys. Finally we here a voice yell out, "Quit fighting like a damn married couple."

We stop dead in our tracks and look around to find where the voice came from. It came from no other than the captain.

"Gibbs you have court. I am driving and Green you are

riding in the back."

She grunts and starts to walk out of the room. She is followed by the captain and myself. When we reach the parking garage I drive, the captain in the passengers seat, and Jenni sits in the back. It doesn't take long before the captain starts in.

"Remember what I told you. Just tell them exactly what happened and I am sure they will vote it self-defense. They have to know that you were in an impossible circumstances and that there was not any other choice for you to do what you did," Captain Green states.

I nod my head in agreement and then a thought passes through my head that had not been there for a while.

"Have we had any luck on that man who claimed to be my father on the island?" I question.

"No not yet. I am sure we will find him soon though." The captain says.

"What man?" Jenni asks.

"The man on the island who was supposedly my father. When we got back to the United States he disappeared my first day back to work." I announce.

"I thought...." that is all she gets out before her father interrupts her.

"We are here. Gibbs you need to focus on one thing at a time."

Maybe he is right. I should focus on one thing at a time. Then maybe just maybe I can start crossing that long list of things to do off. Right now I got two million things on that list hopefully sooner rather than later I can at least cross one million of that off.

I park the car and get out. I am met by Sarah who has an angry facial expression.

"Do you not care if you go to jail or not?" she yells.

"I made it on time," I snare back.

"Yeah with about thirty seconds to spare. Now get in there and take care of this."

Every day she sounds even more like her mother. Shyanne was a caring and loving woman, but when you piss her off just watch out there is a tornado coming through. And it will not stop until she makes you feel like complete shit.

I rush into the court room and walk before the judge. There is no lawyers involved. There is just the judge, my family and friends, and me. Well there of course is the press waiting outside for the verdict to see if one of Chicago's finest will go down in smoke.

The judge I go before today is fairly new to the job. He just earned his chair last year, which in a way kind of scares me. This is really his first big case of any sort and its really not even a case. It is more of just a hearing to see if I could be facing time or if they are not going to trail about it.

The judge is short bulky man. He is probably around the same age I am and has a scar above his right eyebrow. Rumor has it that before he became a judge he was a marine. When he was in war he became a prison of war and that mark is the memory of it. It was said that he was put in a camp surrounded by one hundred foreign soldiers. He always told everyone that there was only four prisoners and that the five of them manage to fight their ways out of it. All he had to show for it was his battle scar.

"Mr. Gibbs, how are you doing today?" the judge asks me.

"Depends how today goes, Your Honor," I respond respectfully.

"Well, you tell me the truth and I am sure everything will just go perfectly fine," he states with a smile.

I nod my head to symbol that I understand what the judge says.

"Go ahead whenever you are ready Mr. Gibbs."

I sit there explaining the events that happened on the island for hours until I finally reach the end of the story.

"This man you say is your father. Is he here today to verify what happened?"

"No sir. When we got back to the States I lost contact with him, and we have not been able to track him down ever since," I announce.

He writes down the notes that I say to him one after one. I think I have seen him start a new piece of paper about five times now. He finishes writing the last words and then places his pen on the desk before him. He takes of his reading glasses and then looks my way.

"Mr. Gibbs. I will not make you wait around for an answer today because I know you are a busy man with the cases that are on your plate right now. I do want to to say something though first. Scott Frost was a terrible and evil man. The world is a better place without him. I know a person of my high rank should not be saying things like this, but you did your country a great service by killing him. So, without further a due I find that there will be no charges held against Mr. James Gibbs in the cases of the murder of Scott Frost. I am ruling that the murder was acted upon in self-defense. Do you agree with my ruling Mr. Gibbs?"

"I do, Your Honor."

"I figured you would. Now get out there and catch this killer that they calling "The Chevy Killer." For I have heard the news of Frosts copy cat. May you bring justice to him. I suggest that you guys use the back exit. I heard that the lobby was full of the press."

He then slams down his gavel and leaves the room. I stand there for a moment trying to comprehend what the judge told me to do. It almost sounds as if the judge told me to kill The Chevy Killer just as I did Frost. I am not going to lie I have thought about doing that many times. Definitely after he threaten my family and I. Still at this point and time that is the plan that intend on going through with.

~Chapter 21~

I SET MY ALARM and lay down in my bed. My eyes drift off into darkness and moments later I am snoring. Tonight must be crazy dream night because the ones I am having so far are strange. The first couple I was already use to because I had haven them before in visions.

I don't understand why I am still having Frosts memories flowing throughout my head. The doctors said that those should be long gone out of my system and there is no reason for me to continue seeing them either.

No matter what that doctor says though I am still having them. And lately they have been growing in intensity. The vision show more each time and show more juicy details. None of which though lead to why I am still having them.

Like I said before though those dreams are normal to me. The dream though that I am having right this minute is completely unfamiliar and frightening to me. I am walking down the street when these two people who look to be in their mid-twenties approach me. One is male and the other is a female. Their faces though are not normal. I am not sure if I am even in the dream at all. Just the point of view I makes me seem like I am seeing it through someone else eyes. The two people approach me closer and I can see their deformed faces. They have wings growing from there backs and their eyes are a solid black. There is no white showing in them at all. Just a soulless pit for their eyes, and they are staring right at me. They come running at me and trying to attack the person I am seeing through for some reason. Or at least that is how it seems. The person though I can see through puts a stop to it quickly when he/she pulls out a sword. One much like the one Frost presented me on the island and kills the two people.

I wake up yelling at what I just seen. Frost has planted his memories of all of his killings inside of my head. Maybe this is his plan after everything. He knows I have a heart unlike him and he knew by me killing him it would draw me mad. Just to spice up the game he made and accomplish before he let me kill him and somehow planted all these memories in my damn head.

A few seconds after I wake up Sarah comes running from the living room. She runs right through the door panting when she reaches her destination.

"What is wrong?" she pants.

"Just a really bad dream."

"Want to talk about it?"

"Not really," I say aloud. "But those eyes where demonic," I whisper to myself.

I thought I said it soft enough for only my ears to hear, but I was wrong. Sarah too heard what I said.

"What eyes?"

Well, the cat is out of the bag now. I mise as well tell her. I do just that along with explaining what Frost did to me. She sits there for a couple minutes trying to figure out everything I just said.

"Maybe you should see a therapist about this," she insist.

"That is why I am talking to you. I can get answers from you for free. Why would I pay for someone who is dumber than you dear?"

She laughs for a minute, but it doesn't take long before she is back on her mission.

"Do it for me please dad. you are all that I have left," Sarah pleads.

Oh hell no she did not just play that card on me. That is the oldest card in the playbook. With her being my only child and only the second girl I ever loved she knows it will work every time.

"Fine. I will go to one sessions and see how I like it. I make no promises on any more."

"Thank you, daddy," she says as she reaches in and gives me a kiss on the check. she then walks towards the way out of the room.

"I love you and goodnight. I'll see you in the morning," I tell her.

"I love you too," she replies as she closes my bedroom door.

I lay back down in my bed and look over at my clock. It read one-fifteen a.m. I then close my eyes and pray that I never have a crazy dream like that again.

~Chapter 22~

JENNI AND I wait for the elevator doors to open. They open at the basement level and then proceed out. We walk up to a glass door that reads, *Dustin Jones M.E.*. Well we are in the right place for sure.

Early this morning about two a.m. Mr. Jones called me and told me when I came in this morning to come immediately top him. That he might have a clue or something about the murders.

We walk through the door and there Mr. Jones is. He is examining a body they found in the river this morning.

"Any connection?" Jenni asks.

"I doubt it. It looks like a gang killing," Jones answers.

"That is a good thing then," she states. We both look at her with a look like you didn't just say that. I guess she realized what she said because now she is trying to explain her reasoning. "I meant that The Chevy Killer has not attacked again."

"Mhm," I tell her. "What do you got for us Jones?"

"Oh yes," he states as he put his materials down on the table. He then walks over to a desk that has evidence on it. He grabs two bags that are labeled Hunter James and Brittany Johnson.

"Look at this," he says.

He hands the bags to us. One to Jenni and one to me. The bag appears to have a bullet in it.

"Congratulations Jones you found bullets. We already knew the victims had been shot though," I announce to him as I start to hand him the bag again.

Instead of him taking the bag, he hands me a pair of gloves. I look at them for a minute and then finally I grab them from his hands.

"I found it when I was trying to find the serial number for the bullet," Jones states.

"That is not in your job description!" Jenni exclaims.

I ignore them for a minute even though I still hear them battling back and forth. I tone them out and pour the bullets on the table. I then take a scoop and look closely at the bullets. It takes me a second to find what Jones found, but when I do I stop in shock.

The two of them are still fighting when I go back to them.

"Will you two just shut the hell up!" I yell.

"No I will not. He could have tampered with the evidence and you don't seem to care."

"He has been doing stuff like this for years. He is careful and doesn't fuck up anything," I snare back at her before continuing. "And before you go and try to tell your father he knows of this too."

She stops talking and puts her head down.

"Besides if it wasn't for Mr. Jones here it would have taken weeks for us to get the information that he just provided us with."

"Well, what do we got?" Jenni questions.

"The bullets that he find in the victims they have the names Hunter James and Brittany Johnson carved into the side of them. Meaning the victims were probably being stocked for weeks," I declare.

"I believe it is time to go to see Mrs. James. Maybe she knows more about her husbands possible affair than what she was leading off. We need to find out what she knows." I say.

"There is one more thing." Mr. Jones adds in.

"Whats that?" Jenni questions.

"There was semen found in the woman's vaginal area. I had it sent over to the lab for testing. I just thought I would let you know."

"Thank you. If you find anything else out please let my partner or I know," I state.

~Chapter 23~

JENNI AND I WALK up to Mrs. James door. Jenni knocks and we wait for Mrs. James to answer. After a few dozen seconds. A middle age woman with long, curly, black hair comes to the door.

"Detectives," she says.

We have already been here once before to notify the family of their lose. You would think after so many times of doing this you would get use to the pain of telling families that their loved ones had just died. You never do though. Most of the time it gets harder on you instead and weighs you down in guilt. Mrs. James is holding her two year old son in her arms.

"Have you found out any more information about my husbands death?" she questions us.

"A few things. Do you mind if we come in and talk in private?" Jenni explains.

"Certainly."

She opens the door completely and we walk into the house. The house is pretty damn big if I must say so. That of course is to be expected. her late husband was a professional football player. On top of that he was a pretty damn good ball player. She shows us back into the living room where we sat the last time that we were her.

"Can I get you any tea or anything?"

"Yes please," I announce.

"I'm going to take my son upstairs and then get us some drinks."

I nod my head in agreement as Jenni and I watch her leave the room. I am a little uneasy about letting her walk around by herself after what happen with Mrs. Johnson. When Mrs. James leaves out of sight I scurry around the room to see if there are any clues at all.

"Do you really think that she knew about the possibly affair?" Jenni asks me.

"You never know in this line of work. Sarah did say that it was all over the television. Unless Mrs. James is against televisions I am sure she knows if there is any truth to it," I answer.

"What are you going to do if we find out she did know?"

I don't get a chance to answer her before Mrs. James enters the room carrying a tray with a pitcher of tea and three glasses on it. She lays the tray on the table in the middle of the room and pours everyone a drink. When she finishes she sits down on the couch across from Jenni and I.

"So, what news do you have for me?"

"Well, there was a bullet found with your husbands name on it. Meaning that more than likely whoever killed your husband knew who he was."

"That only narrows it down to a couple million people. He is a very popular athlete, detective," Mrs. James answers swiftly.

"Yes we know. Which gets to my point of had anyone been making any threats to your husband in the days leading up to his death?" I ask.

"No nothing out of the ordinary. We received death threats all the time from opposing team fans. But nothing was ever serious."

"We are going to need to see all of those threat if that is possible."

"Yes sir. We saved everything just in case. I will have that arranged to be sent to the station before the end of the day."

"Thank you," Jenni proclaims.

There is a gigantic silence throughout the room for a little while. We sat there awkwardly as we watch each other drink from our glasses. My glass empties and I place it back on the tray.

"Can I get you any more?" Mrs. James asks.

"No thank you," I reply.

"Is there anything else that has came to light in the case?"

I take a huge gulp before opening my mouth.

"There is one more thing," I say with a fear in my voice.

Mrs. James just wait for me to ask the question so that she can answer us.

"We have reason to believe that your husband had been having an affair with the other victim. Did you know about this?" I question.

Mrs. James continues to remain silent and from all of the expressions she has I already know the answer. For a woman who just found out her husband was cheating on her she is pretty calm. Which now leads me to believe that she did in fact know.

"Yes that is true," Mrs. James answers.

I look over at Jenni and she looks back at me waiting for a response to what Mrs. James just told us.

"Mrs. James we will be in touch. We will have some follow up questions that you might have to come down to the station for. So, please don't leave town," I tell her.

"I have nothing to hide detective. So, you have my word I will not be going anywhere."

I wouldn't either if I lived in a house like this. Even if I did just become the number one suspect in my husbands murder case. Mrs. James leads us out the door. We walk to our car and get in.

"You believe she did it don't you?" Jenni asks me.

"I don't know, but it is not looking good for Mrs. James. There is one thing though I have learned in my twenty-five years of service."

"What is that?"

"Never be to sure of anything. The moment you become

that something will come up and bite you in the ass with a surprise."

Jenni and I laugh about it for a moment and then we pull out of the drive.

"Where do you want to go eat at for lunch?" Jenni asks.

"I know a place, not to far from here. It is just on the outskirts of the city limits," I reply.

"Good, I am starving," she states with a smile.

~Chapter 24~

WE PULL INTO A Japanese restaurant parking lot. I put the car into park and we walk through the front door. Tokyo is the name of this restaurant.

I love eating here even though it has been little over three years since I last ate here. In fact the last time I ate here was with my wife and the first just the same. This is even the place I proposed to my wife at. So, I really can't wrap my head around why I said we should eat here. It is like I am spitting in her face by bringing another woman here. Even though Jenni is just my partner at work.

"How many?" The host says.

"Two please. And could we get an area where it is private. We are detectives and we would like privacy to discuss our cases," I ask the young woman.

"I can certainly make that happen," she laughs.

We follow her to the back area of the restaurant. Finally we reach our table where no one else is even visible to us. This is the VIP seats. I only know this because this is the section where I did the proposal at. We were not in the same seats, but pretty darn close. Back here the chefs come out and cook the food out in front of you.

We give the waiter our orders and she goes back to the kitchen to get a chef to prepare everything. The waiter brings me our drinks. Usually I would have a beer or something, but since i am on duty I am not allowed to.

"So, Mrs. James." Jenni randomly says.

"What about her?"

"Do you really think she did it?"

"I am not sure, but we can't rule her out at all. If she knew about her husbands affair then she could have a great reason to murder the victims. I have seen people get murder over less. There was this one case that I had about five years ago. You might have heard about it because your father and I worked it together. These two business men had been in a poker game. The game was not for money or anything. They were just friends playing with chips for fun. Well, what supposedly happened was that one of the men thought he got cheated. So, two days later the other business man turned up dead. It didn't take long for us to catch the criminal. To be honest we didn't catch him. He turned himself in. I tell you this story because anyone is capable of murder. Someone else just has to hit their breaking point," I state.

"I don't think that is true. I believe murder is a choice and the killer has all the control. If they wanted to stop they could," Jenni explains.

"That is your opinion and you heard mine."

"And what you said about everyone is capable that is not true either. You have no breaking point, James. If you were going to break you probably would have already."

"I didn't break, but I did kill Frost."

"In self-defense."

"Still killing a person, either to protect yourself or not, murder is murder," I declare.

She sighs and just in the nick of time. The chef comes out and I recognize him immediately. I just hope he doesn't remember me. He is the chef that was there the night I proposed. Now every time he sees me he doesn't let me forget.

"Detective Gibbs," the Asian man says.

I smile on the outside, but inside I am giving him a death stare.

"How have you been?" I ask just to be polite.

"Still at this dreadful place," he laughs.

"Is this your daughter?" He questions.

"No, this is Jenni Green, my new partner at work."

He reaches out his hand and she shakes it back.

"Nice to meet you," she says.

"You too."

"Well, how is the wife? I still remember that night you proposed to her," he states happily.

I say nothing and stare down at the ground. Jenni puts her hand on my shoulder and tells me its going to be okay.

"Did I say something wrong?" the chef asks.

"No, its just my wife has passed away."

"I am really sorry to hear that detective."

"It is okay. To be honest that is the first time I have said it out loud," I declare. That is the complete truth because Sarah was the one who notified all of the people who attend Shaynne's funeral. I tried once and I couldn't seem to say the words. They say you feel better when you confront the death. I think that is bull shit because I still feel the same. That just my opinion though.

We wait for the food to finish and then we dig into our plate.

"Thank you," I tell the cook.

"Your welcome. Hope to see you soon," he smiles.

~Chapter 25~

I WALK THROUGH the doors of the therapist building. I look to my right at a sign that reads all of the business that are available in this building. There is food and coffee places. There is a little gift store on the second level. The business I am going to though is on the fourth floor and is called Challenger's Therapy.

The therapist name is Guy Challenger. That is where the business name comes from I guess.

I really didn't want to come to this, but I told Sarah that I would. And with everything that has happened lately I don't want to let her down. I only agreed to at least one visit though. So, if I don't like it I don't have to stay. With the way prices are I wouldn't want to come back either. For a one hour session it is costing me two-hundred and fifty bucks. Maybe I went into the wrong profession.

"I am here to see Mr. Challenger," I tell the secretary.

"Do you have an appointment?"

"Yes, ma'am. My name is James Gibbs."

She looks up from her computer screen for a second.

"You are the detective that killed Scott Frost right?"

"Yeah that is me."

She smiles without saying any response. Ever since I killed Frost it is as if I became my own celebrity myself. My name was all over the television for weeks afterwards. It just died down about yesterday with all the hype.

"Go through the door and his office is the first room on

the right. He will be right in," the secretary says.

"Thank you."

I do the exact directions that the woman gave me. When I reach his office the door is wide open. I would knock but there is no door to knock on. So, I just walk into the room and sit down in the normal chair. I say normal chair because on the other side of the room there is another chair, that is flat out where you can lay down. You know the one I am talking about like how they always show in the movies a therapist having. Well, this is not the movies and the chair is really in the room.

I really could use a nap right now. I rather do that than talk to this guy. Once again though, I tell myself, you promised your daughter.

I have been here for about five minutes and about ready to leave when the therapist walks through the door. He has a nerdish look to him with red, curly hair. I can't help but to think this guy had to get made fun of during his high school years. That is probably why he became a therapist in the first place because he needed it first.

If you haven't notice by now I am very judgmental, but most of the time my hunches are correct.

"Hello, I am Mr. Challenger," he states.

That was a little weird that he didn't put a doctor in front of his name. Maybe that is just a movie thing that they do that.

"Mr. Gibbs."

Mr. Challenger laughs right away. Did I miss something because I know of nothing that is funny. I try not to be an ass about it when I ask what he is laughing about.

"You are the first person that has walked through my door that noticed I didn't put doctor in front of my name. Everyone else I have to tell them later in the session," he answers.

How in the hell did he know that was what I am thinking. I know for a fact that I didn't say it out loud.

"And now you are thinking of how I figured out what you were questioning," he states, pauses and then continues. "I am very good with facial expressions. And your face tells me anything."

I turn around and sit back down in my chair. As I do so I think to myself creep show. I make sure the therapist can't see my face though. Mr. Challenger comes around to his desk and sits down in his chair.

"So, I have reviewed all of the information you gave me over the phone," he states.

I hear what he is saying, but I am not paying attention. I am still shocked at how he figures out what I am thinking. That and when he entered the room there was no door closing. Once again because there is no door at all.

"Hold on a second. What is with the door? Why is there not one?" I declare out loud.

Mr. Challenger laughs out loud for a moment and then he begins to answer my question, "We have an open door policy. Whenever you feel the need to come in or call for a short conversation we allow it."

"Of course for a price right?" I chuckle.

"As long as the meeting doesn't last over ten minutes then no there is no price. Speaking of money though you are wasting yours now. You came here to talk about you. So lets get started. As I was saying before and I have reviewed your file. There is plenty of reasons for you to be having problems," he answers.

"Gezz, you get straight to the point don't you?"

"Well, I thought you being a detective and all you would like for me to get straight to the point. I guess I was wrong."

"No, you are fine."

He pulls out a piece of paper and a pen. Then he gives me a sharp look and asks for me to start telling everything that has happened. I do exactly what he asks and then when my time is up I leave.

~*Chapter 26*~

I WAKE UP TO my phone going crazy off the hook. I reach over on my night stand and grab it. It is Jenni calling. I click the accept button even though I really don't want to. As I do so I look at the clock and it reads 2:32 a.m.

"It is two thirty in the morning. This better be good," I answer the phone directly.

"About damn time. Everyone has been trying to get a hold of you for about an hour now. You better get up and get dressed," she exclaims.

"Why?"

"Looks like The Chevy Killer just hit again," she says.

I hang up the phone and immediately get dressed. It has only been about three weeks since we found the first bodies. Whoever this guy is he is striking fast. Most killers plan out everything and then do what they need to with patience. They feel in control so they feel no rush at all.

I run through the living room and past Sarah who is doing paper work for her company. Well almost company. She is suppose to sign the papers next week.

"Got to go. I'm in a hurry. Love you," I yell.

I don't eve give her a chance to respond when I slam the

door. I hurry down to my truck and hit my sirens. I take of in a rush dashing and weaving between traffic.

I gather my thoughts still in a hurry to get where I am going when I realize that I am not sure where the murder scene is. I pull out my phone and dial Jenni's number. She answers after two rings.

"Yes?" she states.

"Where are you at?" I question.

"I was waiting for you to call back. Under the bridge in the projects," she laughs.

I hang up the phone and turn around because I am going the complete opposite way. There is only one bridge in the projects and unfortunately for me I have been there many times. A lot of the gangs like to dump their victims there.

Jenni said it was The Chevy Killer though and not a gang beef. How is she so sure of that though?

I really need to stop doing that because as I pull up I too understand why it is The Chevy Killer's work. Tied up to the bridge is a female and a male. Just like before the victims had been cut up and sewed back together. And a bullet hole is placed in either one of their heads. In between the two dead corpses is the words once again painted in blood, *Do you like my work, Detective Gibbs?*

I lower my head and watch as they cut down the bodies.

"Did they get everything before lowering the bodies?" I question Jenni.

I would have wanted to cut them down immediately, but I know that we couldn't because it would tamper with the crime scene. That is the only reason I ask her.

"Yes. Well at least we know that Mrs. James is not The Chevy Killer."

"We can not rule that out yet still. She could have had some kind of mental break after killing her husband. I want you to have an officer go and pick her up for questioning right away!" I exclaim.

She nods her head and then head over to her car to call in what I asked. As she does so I walk over the bodies and try to examine them before the corner comes over. After I get every bit of information I can I look back at the words that are painted on the bridge. After the first murders I was questioning whether or not it was my fault. After these two victims though, I now know that it is my fault.

"See what we can pull up on our two victims please," I yell to Jenni.

~Chapter 27~

WE PULL BACK into the station and begin to sort through the information on the two new victims. The male victim is names Jake Moore. There not much to tell about him. He has no address listed and no place of employment. To be honest, we were lucky to even find out his name. The only reason we did is because he had a record from being in jail from two years ago. He had a public intoxication back in the area that we found the victims. He was dressed with ragged and torn clothes. From the looks of it he had not changed anytime soon. All the evidence pointed to the man being homeless.

The female victim goes by the name of Hannah Mickelson. This victim is completely opposite of the other one. She was dressed in nice professional clothes. Her hair smells of roses (probably from her shampoo or cologne.). She is married to another man that is just as wealthy looking as her.

From everything we looked at so far there is nothing in common with the two victims at all. I haven't had the chance to put the other two victims in the equation yet. I had to put another detective on that part.

I slam the paper down and I see everyone in the room turn their attention towards me.

"These victims have absolutely nothing in common at all. It is like The Chevy Killer is going around just killing random people," I announce.

Jenni walks over to me and puts her hands on my shoulders. She begins to massage my shoulder and calm my nerves. Everyone draws their attention back to what they were doing before.

"We also said that about Mr. James and Miss Johnson. And we found a connection didn't we?" Jenni asks.

"Yeah," I reply.

I am toning out because the massage she is giving me feels so good. She is right though. It has only been about five hours since we began looking. The other two victims took weeks for us to find a connection.

I am usually the one who has patience, but not with this case though. Everything about it stretches my nerves to the point where I want to snap. From Frosts' first murder twenty five year ago to now this copy cat killer, that seems ten times worse than Frost ever was. I see why he is calling himself The Chevy Killer. It's because he is rolling through victims like it is nothing. This complete opposite of Frost. He took his time with it all, but not his prodigy.

"Come on lets go grab something to eat and ease our minds. When we get back with a fresh head maybe we will be able to see something we didn't before," Jenni explains.

I think about it for a minute or two. I don't need to, but it's a good idea to retrain my brain for about an hour or two.

"Okay, come on."

I grab my jacket and we begin to walk out the door. Just as we reach the door we are stopped by another detective that is helping us work the case.

"I found something," he states.

"We are going to clear our minds. Let me know it when I get back."

"I think you might want to hear this now," the detective declares.

I raise my eyebrows because usually in our line of work when someone says that phrase then that means they have something good.

"Alright, what is it?"

"The male victim, Jake Moore, is Mrs. James little

brother," he announces with a smile on his face.

I too smile a great deal because now not only do we have a connection between these two victims, we have a connection between all the victims. I run to my desk slam my jacket back on my chair and start walking out of the room again.

"Where are you going?" Jenni asks.

"Mrs. James is down in the interrogation room right?"

"Yeah."

Then that is where I am going. You can gladly follow along."

She runs to catch up as I hit the stair way. We scurry down the stairs until we get to the first level. We rush down the hallway to the first interrogation room where Mrs. James is located at. I open the door. Instead of rushing in like I have been for the past several minutes I stop almost immediately. There is blood dripping out of Mrs. James neck as her head lays down on the table. Behind her body reads the words, *Wrong connection. Yours Truly, The Chevy Killer.*

I run over to the other chair across from Mrs. James dead body and sling it across the room at the message in complete rage.

~Chapter 28~

I WALK UP THE stairs to the captains office immediately after finding Mrs. James dead body. I storm right through the door without giving Tara and him any warning. They are doing their usually thing. She quickly gets dressed and runs out of the room.

"What the hell, James!" he exclaims.

"We got a big fucking problem," I state.

"What is it?" he responds as he adjusts his clothing.

"Mrs. James is dead. We found her in the interrogation room with her neck sliced," I demand.

I expect a concern or even a little bit of worried look to be on his face, but I see nothing. I see his same old non-emotional facial expression that he always has had on. In the past twenty-five years of knowing him I never known it to change.

"Did we see anyone leave the room?" Captain Green asks.

"No one was even near the room when we came down to talk to her. And get this the Jake Moore guy that we found early this morning he is Mrs. James brother. We thought she was the killer, but now that she has fell victim too we are back to no leads at all," I explain to him.

"What about the footage? We have cameras in those

rooms. I am sure they picked up something."

I had completely forgot in all of the commotion about checking the cameras for evidence first.

"I am going down there right now," I state.

I don't give him time to respond before I start leaving the room.

"Wait," he says.

I turn around to face him again. He is grabbing his jacket and is walking my way.

"I am going with you!" he exclaims.

I nod my head in agreement as we walk out of the room. We take the elevator to the basement. Most of the time the only reason I come down here is to see Mr. Jones. There is one other room though that is in the basement, the security office. I know sounds a little strange to have one in a police station, but things happen inside a station and we need camera for it. Prime example is right now we could catch a killer.

There was another time though we had to use it. It was on a rookie detective who lost his temper with one of the suspects. The suspect was a man from one of the gangs and he knew how to get under peoples skin. I wanted to punch him a couple dozen times, but didn't. This rookie detective though, was young much like Jenni and didn't yet know how to control his anger. So when the suspect started talking about certain things that he would like to do to the detectives' girlfriend the officer lost it. He got a good ten or eleven punches in before anyone was able to get in there to stop him. The suspects face looked like a package of raw hamburger meat when the detective finished with him.

We had to lock the detective up in a holding cell for a night. The next day he was awarded with a prize for having the courage to shut the guy up. We have had problems with that suspect for years and until then no one had stood up to him. Ever since that day we have no longer had any problems out of that suspect. Unfortunately, for the rookie detective no one has seen him since that day either. Ten minutes after receiving the award he also was handed his termination papers.

So, my point being, these cameras come in handy sometimes. For good or bad. Hopefully in this case though, it will help us catch The Chevy Killer.

We knock on the door and after getting a response from the guard in the room we enter. When we do a heavy set man stands up from his chair. He has his mouth stuffed with a donut. Gezz thank you for helping the stereo type out about us cops.

He tries to hurry as fast as he can to swallow the food. Finally, he does and then asks us, "What can I do for you guys today?"

"We need to see the footage of interrogation room for the past couple hours," the captain says.

"Okay that is doable," the guard laughs as he sits back down in his chair.

He brings up the footage of the room on a bigger screen. He rewinds it back a little bit. Then he begins to fast forward it slowly. We see Mrs. James being brought into the room. Then it continues on for a while its just her doing random shit to pass time I guess. Finally, the door opens about an hour ago from now. A person with black clothing comes into the room. The person keeps his/hers head down away from the camera. We watch as The Chevy Killer walks closer to a frighten Mrs. James and the killer slices her neck. We also watch as the person places the words on the wall from Mrs. James blood. The killer then goes back to the table and grabs a piece of paper off the table beside Mrs. James. He then takes some more of her blood and begins to what appears to be writing something again. Then the killer walks back to the door, but stops before exiting. He/she keeps their head down as they raise the piece of paper up in front of the camera. *Game On, Pigs,* it reads. The person holding the paper then raises their head. When they do the mystery person is still a mystery because the person is wearing a clown mask. In the slot where the mouth goes you can see The Chevy Killer crack a little smirk. The killer then walks out of the room with swagger.

The guard then switches the cameras back to the hallway and when he does we see that the killer throws the piece of paper away in the trash can. The captain and I immediately look up at each other. I take off running out of the room to the hallway where the piece of paper was thrown away.

When I was watching the tape I notice that the killer was not wear gloves for some reason. So, since he threw that paper away and he had his hands on it that means we have finger prints. I run into the hallway where the trash can is at. When I reach my destination the janitor is picking up the trash from the area. It just so happens he is picking up the bag I need now.

"Stop," I echo throughout the hallway.

The janitor drops the bag in shock as I approach him. I open the bag and dig through it for the piece of paper. I can see the janitor giving me a strange look out of the corner of my eye.

"Sorry we have evidence in here," I try to explain

The janitor gives me a look like yeah sure okay, whatever you say man.

I ignore the look with no response and I continue to dig. Finally about half way down I locate the damn thing. I, of course, have my gloves on so all of the nasty shit doesn't bother me. I grab the piece of paper and read it to make sure it is the right one. Sure enough it is. I stand back to my feet and start to walk away.

"Where are you going?" I hear.

I turn around and look. The janitor is the one speaking to me.

"I am going to the lab to get the finger prints off of this," I state.

"Aren't you going to clean his mess up you made?" he asks.

I look down at the hallway floor where I made a complete mess of all the trash from that bag.

"You are the janitor. That is your job not mine," I snare.

I then turn back around and head towards the lab. I stop once more and tun back at the janitor.

"When I get done with this I will buy you lunch while I am waiting on the results. Does that sound fair to you?" I ask him.

"Yeah.," he answers.

I did make a mess so I guess I will make the guys day a little easier since I already made it harder. I then clear my mind and begin to walk to the lab for the final time. I am on my way to find the name of the killer who has been haunting me. I am one step closer to putting an official end to the Frost legacy.

~Chapter 29~

I BARGE THROUGH the door of the lab.

"I need this examine right away," I yell.

"You will have to tag it in and wait for it's turn," the lab technician states.

He then goes back to doing what he was doing before. I walk over to the lab rat and grab him up by his collar.

"You are going to examine this right now. It is very important," I announce.

"Okay," he mumbles.

I hand him the sample and tell him all I need is a finger print. Then I tell him to call me as soon as he gets the results. He nods in agreement and I storm out of the room.

I then proceed back to the hallway where I found the piece of paper. I find the janitor that I pissed off before, and I walk up to him.

"Are you ready?" I question.

"To go where?"

"To lunch. I told you I would take you."

"Oh you don't have to do that sir. Everything is fine. Besides my lunch isn't for another hour and a half."

"Non-sense, let's go. I will take care of the captain if he says something about it," I declare.

He puts his mop down and begins to think. Finally, after

a few minutes he agrees and we take off out the door. We walk across the street to the parking garage. We hop in the car and begin to drive down the road.

After about five minutes of silence I break it.

"So, what is your name?"

"Johnny Cash."

I look over at him with a strange look.

"Like the singer?" I question.

"Just like him. My mother had a crush on him when she was younger. From day one of hearing him, she said she would always name her child that. I have two younger brothers and you wouldn't guess their names," Mr. Cash says.

"Don't tell me" I pause. "Hank and Willie."

"Close, but no. Hank and Waylon," He laughs.

"That was my next guess."

We pull up to the Tokyo restaurant that Jenni and I ate at a couple weeks ago. This week is the same except Jenni and I drove separate and we are going to have Mr. Cash tagging along this time. When we pull into the parking lot I don't see Jenni's car. We wait for a little bit and she still hasn't pulled up yet. We give up on waiting and then we decide to walk inside.

We find our normal seats. For thirty minutes straight we find random shit to talk about. Mostly about his past and how he feels about his name. About thirty minutes later Jenni finally joins us. I stand up and kiss her on the check when she walks through the door.

"What took so long?"

"I was hoping to find out the results of the finger prints labs before I came to lunch," she states.

"Anything yet?" I question.

"No, They said it would at least be another two hours."

"Of course. Well have a seat."

Before she sits down though I introduce her to Mr. Cash. She immediately laughs, and then begins to explain to how her grandmother is related to her in some long distance way. We try to process it all, but we can't. Instead of telling her we can't understand what she is trying to explain we just nod our heads acting like we know what she talking about.

"So, Mr. Cash how old are you?" Jenni asks.

From the looks of him he is about twenty five. He is from Kentucky though and from what he has told me he has been working since he was about fifteen.

"I am eighteen," he states.

I spit up my food to his response. There is no way in the world he is eighteen. He is way to mature and doesn't look the part at all. I wipe my face of the chewed up food.

"I am sorry did you say eighteen?" I question.

"Yeah,"

"You could have fooled me," I state.

"Not sure which way to take that, but thank you," he laughs back.

Jenni and I laugh right after him. Seconds later my phone begins to ring. I look at the caller ID and it is the lab.

"Hello," I answer.

"Detective Gibbs?" the lab rat says over the phone.

"Yes."

"We got your results back."

"And what are they?" I ask him.

"I think you should come back to the lab right away. There seems to be a problem," he declares.

"Okay we are on the way. "

I hang up the phone and tell the two others that we need to cut lunch early today. They don't argue and we walk out together.

"I will take Mr. Cash back to the station," Jenni insist.

I agree with her and they start walking towards her car. I head the opposite way of the other two. I reach my car and take my keys to unlock it. When I do, I notice a shining light reflecting off my driver's side window. I turn around to see where the light is coming from. When I do I see the sun reflecting off of something at the top of the parking building across the street. It takes me a minute to realize what the reflection actually was. It was coming from a scope off of a sniper rifle. From the direction it was pointing it is pointing towards Jenni and Johnny.

"Get down," I yell.

They turn around to see what I said. Of course they

couldn't just drop like I told them to do. Just then I see Johnny drop to the ground, and the gun shot echo throughout the block. I dart over there to them.

Jenni is kneeling over Johnny trying to block the blood from escaping Mr. Cash's body. There is tons of blood pouring from his chest where the bullet pierced his skin.

"Call this in," I tell Jenni.

I know this is going to sound really rude, but I can tell that Mr. Cash will not make it and I don't have time to waste at the moment. We are on the outer part of the city and it would take at least fifteen minutes for the EMT to get there. That is just if Mr. Cash is lucky and they are close. And the way that Mr. Cash is losing blood he will be lucky to make it five minutes.

"Where are you going?" Jenni questions.

"I seen where the shot came from. I am going to try to meet the shooter before he escapes," I yell as I already take off running.

I don't have time to wait for her approval. I know this is a long shot, but for some reason I believe this shooting has to do with The Chevy Killer. If it is not the killer itself then it is someone that is helping The Chevy Killer. So, there is no time to waste at all.

~*Chapter 30*~

I DART IN THE direction of the sniper. I have to run across traffic. Even though we are on the outer part of the city it is still a busy road. Especially since all of these restaurants are out here, like Tokyo. I dodge in and out of the busy lanes. The last car I met I should wait for, but I run out in front of it anyways because there is no time to spare. The car barely misses my right leg as the driver honks her horn at me.

I don't turn around to look at her, but I know I am getting a certain finger pointed in my direction. I can't help, but to chuckle a little inside my head when that thought crosses my mind. Finally, I step my foot into the parking garage.

I don't stop to take a breathe even though I could really use it right now. Instead though, I continue on. I do have to stop to look at the poster on one of the walls that gives the levels of all the floors inside this parking garage. There is a total of twenty levels to this garage. I would really like to take the elevator this time since I have gotten use to it a lot at the station. I know though that the sniper more than likely has a car in this garage somewhere and will be driving out this way. I know this because this is the only exit there is in this parking lot garage.

I take off running passing every single parking spot along the way. Level by level I fall victim to finding no one. Maybe, I should have just stayed at the exit. Finally, I reach the top and once again I am disappointed by finding no one. I look around just for a clean second swipe and the same result. This time though I just happen to see something on the door that I came out of to reach the roof.

It is a note in blood like always. The message reads, *Does it bother you that this is the second time today I was right under your noses and you missed me both times. HAHAHA ~The Chevy Killer.*

I open the door and slam it shut repeatedly until the door finally starts coming off its' hinge. I take a breather and then remember about Mr. Cash being shot.

I never really forgot about it. I was just so busy trying to get to this parking lot. Even if I did forget about it, I wouldn't for long because The Chevy Killer wouldn't let me.

He is playing mind games with me and I normal wouldn't let these petty games get to me. This killer though is going around just killing anyone and anything. This makes his sixth victim in about a month.

I walk over to the edge where I am sure the sniper once stood to take out Mr. Cash. Sure enough when I get to that spot and look over the edge, I can see a perfect view of Jenni and Mr. Cash. I see the EMT coming down the road only about a quarter mile away.

"I guess I better get down there and help out in any way I can," I mumble to myself.

I turn around and start to walk, but I don't get my second step before I stop. When I was starting to walk I had my head held low in disappointment. When I was looking at the ground I see something shinny on the rooftop at my feet. I bend down to see what it is. I get closer to the object and when I am fully near the ground that is when I realize what this object is. It is the bullet casing from the sniper.

I don't get to study the piece of evidence long because I am startled by a voice. The voice is neither a woman's or a man's. The voice is under one of those recorders that change the appearance of anyone's voice.

"I believe that I must have dropped that," the voice says.

At first I don't look up because I know who this must be. Well, I have two choices here. It is either just the sniper that killed Mr. Cash. Or The Chevy Killer is the sniper and is one of those killers who like to do everything himself.

"Should have known that you were not going to make it that easy for us and wouldn't just leave this behind. This was a trap all along wasn't it?" I question as I stand up to face the killer.

When I stand up the sniper has the clown mask on. So, whoever was at the station is the same person who just killed Mr. Cash.

"You know you really don't give yourself enough credit, detective. You really are smarter than you look. Unfortunately, you are a danger and you must be executed from this picture," the clown faced person says.

I tilt my head sideways a little to symbol I am thinking about what his next move is. The sniper pushes out his hands against my chest. I know I am screwed as soon as he does it because I was only about a foot away from the edge. I swing my arms forward trying to grab him to come along. I would gladly fall to my death if I can take this evil son-of-a-bitch with me. I unfortunately, am unable to reach any part of him. I feel the back of my foot slap the brick that is right at the edge. I trip over it and fall over. Just as I am falling I see the killer walking away from the seen and picking up the evidence of the bullet shell.

When I go to fall my shirt get caught on something. I am dangling over the area just by my shirt. I know it won't last very long before my shirt completely rips. So, I reach my hand up and grab the object that is holding me up. It is not much, but a least I have a grip on something. I just then do the only other thing I know what to do at the moment, yell for Jenni. I just hope she can hear me yelling. My life depends on it.

~*Chapter 31*~

I PLUG THE GUN shot hole inside Mr. Cash's chest. Damn I really wish James was here right now. He would know what to do. I hear sirens pulling up to my location. This is like music to my ears because I am afraid that Mr. Cash is not going to make it very much longer.

The EMT reached me and ask me to move. They also ask everything that is wrong with the man. I tell them about the gun shot and that Mr. Cash was starting to go into shock, but not for very long. They nod their heads and say thank you.

"Is he going to make it?" I question.

"I give him about a ten percent chance right now," One of the EMT's say.

I stand out of the way as they put Johnny into the ambulance. I watch as they drive away in a hurry and as they do so I hear another noise. It sounds as if someone is calling my name. The further away the sirens get the louder the voice gets. Finally, after about ten times of hearing my name I recognize who is yelling. It is James, but from where?

Last thing he told me was he knows where the shot came from, but he didn't let me know where that was before running off. I look around high because from the sound of the gun it was sniper who shot Mr. Cash. I finally spot James hanging from the side of a parking garage across the street.

"Oh shit," I yell as I begin to run towards him.

I dodge traffic and then when I am to the other side of the street I enter the parking garage. I get about halfway up and I hear a pair of tires squealing from the next level up. When I get about half way up the next level I met the car. Whoever is driving it must be in a hurry and they are paying no attention to me at all in the middle of the drive. They actually speed up when they see me.

I quickly pull out my pistol and begin to fire upon the car. Bang...Bang...Bang. Three shots I get off in a roll. That is all I need because the car starts turning to side. The car starts going the way of the exit off the fifth floor. It hits the barrier and goes flying off the edge. I quickly run over to where the car went off and I watch as the car smashes the ground and blows up.

"Wow, that is some cool ass movie shit," I say to myself not thinking that I just killed someone.

I just stand there for a moment thinking how cool that just was and what a big rush that is going through my veins. That is where I hear a voice yelling at me again.

"Will you hurry up already?" James yells.

Oops I forgot that was the whole reason I was coming up here for. I rush to the rooftop and go to the edge where James is hanging from.

"I am here," I yell to him.

"About time, now pull me up," he states.

He is only about a foot down off the edge. So lucky for me it is not going to be that hard to get him up. Which is a very good thing I am not the biggest girl in the world here and James is not the smallest man there is either.

"Just pull me up to the edge. I will be able to get it from there," he declares.

I nod my head in agreement and reach down for him. It is a really good thing that he is not that far down or I wouldn't have been able to reach him. I grab his hand and struggle to get him up, but a few puffs I am able to get him to the edge. He pulls himself the rest of the way up and we fall to the rooftop ground. We laugh for a second.

"I am taking you out to dinner tonight," he says.

I just laugh again to symbol that was fine with me. Then I remember the exploding car.

"Did you see that shit?" I ask him.

"How could I not? I had nothing else to look at. While you were out playing chicken with cars some of us where hanging around," he laughs.

We both get up and start to walking back down the levels of the parking garage. When we reach the bottom we walk over to the now burned out car. The firefighters had already put out the flames and we are surrounded by CPD. We approach the car slowly.

"Time to see who our mystery killer is," I state.

James opens the drivers' side door and out falls out a body. Unfortunately, for us the body is completely burned up. So, there is no knowing of who it is. From the short hair though and the muscle tone it is probably a male. We have waited this long though, what is another couple of days going to hurt? Before we leave the scene we pop the trunk to see what goodies the sniper had in its' trunk. We find the sniper rifle itself and along with it in the case the clown mask. We bag both of them hoping maybe some kind of fingerprints or DNA will show up.

There is one more item that is in the trunk that James seems to paying more attention to than anything else. It is what appears to be a tape recording. James keeps trying to play it from the beginning, but the tape is damage badly. All that we get is a voice that is altered by a device and the voice says, "When the time is right your task is to kill detective Gibbs."

He continues to play it and play it again. Finally, he realizes he is not going to get anymore. He places the tape recorder in a evidence bag and now all he can do is hope that someone back at the station can try to fix the recorder.

James walks over to me and wraps his arms around me.

"I don't know about you, but I think we earned the rest of the day off. So, I will be at your place around eight to get you," he laughs.

At first I am a little confused as what he is talking about and that he is wanting to take the rest of the day off. That is not like James to take a rest.

"For what? And don't you want to wait to see what they get from the evidence?" I ask.

"I told you I was buying you dinner. Besides you know how slow the lab rats are. We probably won't get the results until tomorrow," he states.

I say nothing, but I let out a smile and nod my head. We walk to the car and drive away from the scene.

~*Chapter 32*~

I GET OUT OF the shower, get dressed, and go to my truck. I then proceed to leave the driveway and head towards my destination. Tonight that point is located at 526 Franklin Street, aka Jenni's place.

It doesn't take me very long to get there. Just about ten minutes well maybe a little closer to the eleven minute mark. The only bad thing about this whole thing is, that Jenni still lives with her dad until he been on the job for a little longer. So, I really don't know how this is about to go.

I pull into the drive and put the truck into park. I get out of the car and walk up to the door. I go to knock on the front door, but before I can the door opens. In it's place is Mr. Green. I take a huge gulp and then try to smoothen the mood.

"Hey David," I say.

He says nothing to me and just stares on with a pissed off look on his face. Why is this so hard? I am just taking out my partner for saving my life. It is not it is a date or anything.

"Is Jenni here?" I question.

"Yup."

"I think I am going to go wait for her in the truck. Will you let her know that I am out here?"

"Yup," he says again.

I start to turn around and walk back to my truck.

"What are you doing, James?" he demands.

"Going to my truck," I tell him with a weird look on my face. A look that says I just said that.

"No, I mean with my daughter!" he exclaims loudly.

"Nothing sir," I announce as I turn around to face him. "Your daughter saved my life today out there and I am thanking her by taking her out to dinner is all."

He once again stays silent. So, I turn around and walk towards my truck again.

"James," he interrupts.

"Yeah," I sigh.

"Don't even think about sleeping with her!"

I nod my head and then hop into my truck. I watch as David walks back into the house. About five minutes later Jenni comes storming out of the house. She is yelling at someone, probably her dad. I can't say for sure because I can't hear what she is yelling about. He is probably preaching the same thing that he was to me. She then slams the house door and comes over to the truck.

She gets in and I guess I didn't know how good she looked until now because she was yelling. However though, she looks amazing. She is wearing this beautiful, sexy, red dress and matching lip stick. I just sit there and stare for a very seconds.

"You okay?" she questions as she breaks my concentration.

"Yeah sorry. I was just admiring how beautiful you look tonight is all," I respond.

"Thank you, but keep your hands to yourself. I don't feel like listening to my dad," she laughs.

At least I know who she was yelling at now. I turn my head back to the front. I start the truck and then pull out of the drive.

"So, did you enjoy the rest of your day off?" I question.

"It wasn't to bad. I just laid back and watch some *Netflix*," She responds.

"What did you watch?" I laugh.

"I started a new season. It is called *Arrow*."

"I have watched that it is a really good show. How far did you get?" I answer.

"Just the first episode."

"Well, you definitely need to finish it," I respond.

I continue to drive for about twenty minutes. Then we come to a steakhouse down town. I find the parking area and do what you usually do in a parking lot, park. We get out of the car, and then go into the restaurant.

"How many?" the man at the front says.

"Two," I state.

He takes us to our seat. I pull out Jenni's chair for her and once she is comfortable I take my seat.

"We would like some wine," I say to him.

"Very well."

The waiter walks away and I turn my one hundred percent attention to Jenni. She just smiles her perfect looking smile. We order our food and eat it as well. We thank the server and everyone else involved in the process of our dinner. We go back to my truck and I begin to drive towards her house again.

"Where are you going?"

"I'm taking you home."

"I thought we were going to your place," she states.

"What! I never said that." I answer confused.

"You said we were going to watch *Arrow*."

I really don't remember saying that. I am not going to argue though. Well, then there is always her dad and my boss.

"What about your dad?"

"I am twenty-one years old. I can do what I want. Seems like you are a little scared of him," she laughs.

"He is my boss."

"I can handle my father," she states directly.

"Okay."

I turn the car around and we head to my apartment. If she wants to go to my house I am not going to argue with her anymore about it. She can be the one to deal with her dad though.

We reach my apartment. I go to open the door, but it is locked. No big deal just means that Sarah is not home. She hasn't been home that much lately. She says she has just been sleeping at the office, but Sarah has never been a good liar. I am sure the truth will come out eventually.

We walk in the apartment and I turn some lights on. I

then proceed to lay the keys on the counter. Jenni walks into the bathroom while I go to the bedroom to change.

I finish getting comfortable and walk back to the living room. When I do Jenni is already on the couch. She is in her pjs. She has some short shorts on and a tank top that shows her breast. I have a strange feeling that she was planning this all along.

I then turn on the television followed by the *Play-Station Four* that Sarah has. That is the device we use for our *Netflix*. I then scroll the list of movies and the television shows on it. I really need to put the show on my favorite list so it won't be as hard to find. Finally, I find it and begin to start the show. We decide to watch it from the beginning rather than the second episode. Just to refresh our minds a little bit.

About half way through the first episode I feel Jenni's hand slide over onto my thigh. I pay no attention to it at all. Well, that is at least in the beginning. She begins to move it higher up my leg and I can't help but to notice. I look over at her and when I do she is not paying attention to the movie at all. She is staring at me instead.

"What?" I laugh.

She says nothing and just puts her finger over my mouth to symbolize to shut up. She slowly moves her lips closer to mine and I to hers. After I have a split second of thought I stop.

"We shouldn't do this," I state.

Once again she stays silent. This time she lets out a big smile at me. At first I can't tell what she is smiling at. Well, it doesn't take very long to figure it out because she leans in quickly towards my face. Her lips met mine instantly. We stop after the first touch and then stare in each other eyes. Then we continue on with late night adult activity.

~Chapter 33~

I WAKE UP IN my bed with Jenni laying naked next to me. I reach over and kiss her on her cheek. She wakes up herself and gives me a smile. I then proceed to get up and do my morning pee. When I get out and walk back to the bedroom there Jenni is walking around naked. I let out a big smile that haven't let out in a very long time. This is the closest I have had to feelings since my wife was still alive.

"Good morning," I tell her.

"You too," she replies.

I go back and lay in the bed beside her and we begin to kiss again.

"Are you ready for round two?" she laughs.

I speak of nothing and just continue to answer the question anyways. We get ready to finish when we hear the front door of the apartment open up.

"Dad, you home?" I hear Sarah yell.

An oh shit look comes on both Jenni's and I faces. We hurry to get our clothes on. I don't answer Sarah though because I am to busy.

"Dad, you in here?" she says again as she approaches my bedroom door.

I quickly shove Jenni in the closest. The funny part about it all though is that she only has a bra and panties on. I rush back over to the bed. All I have on is my pants and I am buttoning them up as Jenni walks into the room.

"Dad."

"Yeah I am here," I say breathless.

"I have yelled for you three times now."

"Sorry I was naked and trying to get dressed before you came in," I answer.

That was sort of the truth in a way. I was naked, but that is not the reason I didn't answer.

"Oh," she states.

"Where were you last night?" I question her again even though I will know the answer she will give me.

"At the office again. Last night should be the last time I have to stay there for a while."

"Is everything okay?"

"Yeah. Just finally figure out everything," she tells me.

She begins to walk over to the closest where Jenni is hiding. I dart over in front of her and block her way to the closest.

"What are you doing," I declare.

"Getting some clothes and going to take a shower."

"The closest is a mess right now. I will find them and lay them outside of the bathroom door."

She gives me a strange look and then she pushes me out of the way.

"You are hiding something!" she exclaims.

She then opens the closest and I hurry and go hide behind the bed. I don't know how she will take is when she finds out about this. I kneel beside the bed acting like I am getting something, but my attention of course is completely on Sarah opening that door.

She proceeds to open the closest door and when she does there is nothing, but clothes. A sigh of relief comes across my body, but at the same time a concerned feeling on where the hell Jenni is at. About that time I feel something sliding up my leg and into my pants. I look down and I notice that it is a hand. I know that hand from anywhere it is Jenni. She just happens to go far enough up and I make a moaning noise.

"What did you say?" Sarah says as she turns around to

face me.

I quickly stand up and turn my attention back to my daughter. "I didn't say anything," I quickly reply.

She must have noticed that I was looking down because she is walking my way again. I feel Jenni's hand sliding out of my pants and slither back under the bed. Sarah approaches me and goes straight for the bed.

"What is it that your are trying to hide from me dad?" she investigates.

"Nothing at all," I try to explain to her.

She looks at me and then back to the bed.

"Are you on drugs? Cause if you are it is understandable with everything you have been through lately," she insist.

"Heavens no." I yell immediately.

About that time Jenni comes out of the other side to cover my ass. She stands up tall in her panties and bra with a smile on her face. Sarah takes turn looking back and forth between Jenni and I. Her jaw drops quickly and I am not sure what she is thinking about. Then about five seconds later a smile comes on her face.

"I knew it," she says.

She then goes over to Jenni and grabs her up.

"We have some stuff to talk about," she tells Jenni.

They proceed out of the room leaving me alone with thoughts of what they are talking about. Even though I probably know exactly what she is talking about.

"Women," I state to myself.

~*Chapter 34*~

I WALK INTO the lab hoping for great information, but will probably walk out with disappointment.

"So what was the big problem with the fingerprints?" I ask one of the lab technicians.

He doesn't give me an answer. He just grabs the results of test and hands me the piece of paper. I look down and begin to read it. Well, with all honesty I don't read much of it at all. I just look about half way down where I know the name will be. Two words is all I have to read and I stop. The words read as following, *James Gibbs.*

"What the hell is this?" I question.

"The results, sir."

"I know that. Why in the hell does it have my name on it?"

"That is what came up when we ran it," the lab rat says.

Seconds later in walks Captain Green.

"I am going to have to ask for you to come with me James."

"Why?"

"You know why. Just come with me and we will figure

this all out," he tells me.

I hand the paper back to the lab technician and walk with David back to a interrogation room. I sit down and wait for David to start.

"Must we really do this, David." I question.

"Yes," Green states.

I huff and once again just sit in silence waiting for my old partner to begin. Finally, he opens the folder in front of him. It is very small which is a good thing for me. It just means that the finger prints is the only thing that they have on me.

"Where were you when Mrs. James was murdered?" He asks.

"Up at my desk. Detective Green and I was about to leave when one of the other detectives brought us the information on Mrs. James brother. When we heard about that we immediately went to the room where Mrs. James body was found dead," I formally state.

"So, everyone upstairs can confirm this?"

"Absolutely. That and you can check the cameras again," I declare.

"Thank you for your statement detective. You are free to go," David says.

I stand up from my chair and start to walk out. Once I reach the door I turn back around.

"Do you really believe that I had a part in this?" I question.

"Of course not," he winks.

He joins me as we walk out of the room together. We get back upstairs to his office. He grabs a cigar for both of us. I accept it of course.

"So, I hear that you are going to therapy," he states.

"Yeah. It was something I promised Sarah I would go and try," I answer.

"Oh okay. Well, you heard where the semen DNA came back from both Miss Johnson and Mrs. Mickelson."

"No I hadn't heard that yet. I went straight to the lab this morning."

"Miss Johnson had Mr. James semen in her. So, that just

confirmed the affair that was going on. Here is the weird thing though. Mrs. Mickelson had Mr. Moore's semen in her."

"So, maybe that is the connection. The Chevy Killer was going after people who was having affairs. Would you like me to go question Mr. Mickelson anyways," I question.

"No, they said they should have the DNA back from the man in the burned up car from yesterday by the end of the day," the Captain states.

I nod my head in agreement and finish my cigar. I then thank the Captain for all the information. I proceed to go to the door and back to my desk.

~Chapter 35~

I REACH THE second level of the station. I walk over my desk and sit down right away. I look over some paper work and after a little bit I pick up my telephone and see if I have any voice mails. For those who want to know I don't have any it's just a normal routine to do it though.

My day is brighten up though right at this moment because Jenni just walked through the door and is heading my way. She comes over and sits on my desk.

"Hey there partner," she says.

"Hey Jenni."

"Why did you run off so soon this morning?"

"Needed to get some work done. Plus I don't even want to know what my daughter had to say about her findings this morning," I respond.

"Well, if you must know she actually likes the idea of us being together."

"Together," I stutter.

"Yeah that is what last night meant right."

Don't get me wrong what Jenni and I had last night was amazing. When we are together she is fun and gives my life purpose again. But it has only been about six month since my wife passed away, aka brutally murdered. Then there is the whole situation of our ages and her dad is my boss. I would love the idea of us being together though. I know what I need to tell her, but it is not what I want to tell her.

"We need to take it slow," is what I should say.

Instead the words, "Yeah it is," rolls off my tongue before I can even thinking about stopping it.

"Great, but I think we should keep it kind of secret around work because we don't want anyone starting some bull shit," she declares out of nowhere.

I can't help but to laugh as I agree with her statement. I believe that is the smartest thing to do right now. I have said it many times before and I mean it every time, but none more than now; she is so much more mature than her actual age. Her actual age is twenty-one, but her mature age is about twenty-nine to thirty. So, I guess that would help out for our case a little bit. Besides this world is an entirely different world when it comes to things like that. At least I am not an eighty year old man with a eighteen year old girl.

Jenni gets up off the desk and makes sure she walks her firm ass right in my vision. She grabs her rolling chair from her desk and comes back over to mine. We mise as well get use to sharing things if we are going to be a couple.

"So, what are you looking at?" she asks.

"Just making sure of something is all."

"Okay like what may this certain something may be?"

"You know how we found those finger prints from that man in the car back when he killed Mrs. James?" I answer her question with a question.

"Yeah."

"Well, they found a match for the prints."

"That's great," she states.

Well that was before she looked at the expression upon my face at the moment. After reading that face she starts to speak again.

"Or not."

"The finger prints were mine."

She has confused look on her face. Much like the same one I had when I first found out the results.

"There must be a mistake. You wore gloves didn't you?"

she interrogates.

"Absolutely."

"Then maybe they just messed up the single set of prints."

"There was two sets of prints they said and they both belonged to me. Your father has done my questioning about it. So, I am sure he will be pulling people out asking about my alibi for that time," I try to explain to her.

"You were here with all the other detectives," she yells.

"That is what I told him. He said he would be checking in about it. He is just doing simple procedure in a situation like this," I answer her to calm her down.

She whines about it for a few more minutes and finally I calm her down enough to just drop it. She sits quiet for a minute and then looks at me with a weird look again.

"So, what are you looking for then?"

"I have a theory."

"What may that be?" she tries to convince me into telling.

"I will let you know a little later on. Did you ever happen to find out who owned that island I was kidnapped and placed on by Frost?"

"No, I am so sorry I forgot," she cries.

"It's okay. I will need you to do that this morning though as soon as you can," I state.

"Certainly, babe," she says quiet enough to where only I can hear her.

I crack a smile as soon as the word babe comes out of her mouth. She places her chair back over behind her desk and then comes over to me.

"I am going to go look that up right away. Is there anything else you need me to get?" she asks.

"No thank you. I will see you soon," I respond.

She walks off and out of the door. When I said I will see her soon I meant in probably a couple hours. I definitely didn't mean ten seconds later. She barges back through the door and she is not alone. Her father is right behind her and he doesn't look like he is in a very good mood.

The first thing that crosses my mind is that he found out about Jenni and I last night. I am totally screwed I say internally. I daze out and that is probably best for the yelling I am about to get.

"Gibbs," I hear him yell.

"Yeah," I nervously answer.

"Are you going to join us up here or not?"

I look around at everyone else in the room and they are all gathered around the Captain at the moment. I guess I just didn't notice because I was fearing the worse. I see Jenni waving her hand to tell me to hurry the hell up. I get up from my desk and join the others.

"Thank you," David states.

I nod my head at him as I stand in the front beside Jenni.

"The lab found out who the man was in the car. I want you to get all the information you can on this man, Travis Brown."

The Captain also holds up a picture. I recognize both the picture and the name. I step forward one step closer to the Captain.

"That will not be necessary, Captain," I announce.

"Oh why is that?"

"Because I know this man."

I take a deep breathe as I look around at everyone. I feel Jenni approach my side.

"Who is he?" she questions.

"He is my adaptive father. I can tell you almost anything you need to know about him."

~Chapter 36~

JENNI AND I walk into the Captain's office right behind the Captain himself.

"Tara, I don't want to be disturbed for anything. The three of us are having a very important meeting," he yells at her.

Jenni and I sit down as David slams the door behind us. He walks around to his side of his desk and sits himself.

"Now do you care to explain what the hell you said down there," he directly screams at me.

"Not to sound like a smart ass sir, but I think what I said was pretty clear. I said he is my adoptive father."

"Start from the beginning and don't leave out anything because it could be key to the investigation."

I take a deep breathe and begin my story telling about my second father. Well, to be technical he would be my third father because before I was moved to his house I had another adoptive family. That turned out badly though. The father was a drunk and would abuse me. Finally, after ten years social services caught wind of what he was doing and moved me homes. I was seventeen years old when I met Travis Brown.

Usually when you are that old they would let the kid just stay in the system until turned eighteen and they would never put a child into a new home being that old. They said though that Mr. Brown had been pursuing a child in my position for a while. No one had fit the category in a little bit until I came along.

Mr. Brown is what I called him for the longest time. At first when I met him I knew right away he was going to be a hard ass. After all he is a Sargent Major in the United States Marine Core (USMC). He is the one who got me into the military for four years before I went to the police academy.

When he retired from the military we stayed close and spoke almost everyday. That includes just yesterday before I left my house for work in the morning.

"There is no way that he is the one who did this," I state to David.

"With all do respect James. All of the evidence says otherwise," he responds.

"With all do respect sir! You don't know this man like I do."

"Apparently you didn't know this man as well as you thought you did. If you can find any evidence that he is not linked to this at all I will listen. You have one hour before I go before the press to make the announcement that Travis Brown was the The Chevy Killer," the Captain declares.

"An hour is not enough time to do that," Jenni butts in.

"Then I guess you shouldn't be wasting any of that time sitting here. You are lucky that I am giving you that because I was suppose to meet with them about ten minutes ago."

Jenni and I rush out of the room in a hurry. We go to the elevator and wait for it to meet us.

"I am sorry for your loss," Jenni states.

"Thank you, but it will mean nothing unless we find some sort of evidence freeing him."

We step into the elevator and as I do I begin to have a memory flash of me back in the war. It was back in the seventies. There was no war going on, but just as today we had our special missions. My mission was to save a very important woman over in Russia.

My team and I went into the camp and I lost everyone. I was the last man alive and was completely surrounded by the enemy. That is when shots from no where came and took out the enemy one by one. After the last man fell I found out that I had a secret sniper. That sniper's name was Travis Brown and he saved my life.

I think that is what worries me the most about this all. Knowing that Mr. Brown was a sniper in the USMC and how Mr. Cash died is an easy connection. I just pray that Jenni and I find something to clear his name in enough time before David ruins his name.

"I am sure we will find something," Jenni tells me to calm my nerves.

"I certainly hope so," I tell her as I kiss her on her cheek.

~Chapter 37~

I USUALLY HAVE heard from my father by now today. He must be having a very busy day. No matter though that just means I get a little more me time today. And after everything that has happened lately I could really use that me time.

About two weeks ago I found out that I was pregnant with my first child. The father of my child's name is Randy Rodgers and I am madly in love with him. Unfortunately though, I don't feel that he feels the same about me. Once I told him the great news he took off running.

That is part of the reason I told my dad that I won't be staying the night at the office anymore. Truth is I am not sure how my dad is going to take this when I have to give him this news. So, I have been lying to my dad and saying I been working late a the company office. He seems to be buying the lie. Then again though my dad has always be able to hide his emotions except at my mothers' funeral.

It has been hard on him since that day, but it has been hard on me too. I don't think he realizes how much it has effected me. I went from a young girl who was about to attend Stanford University to taking over my mothers multi-million dollar company. Plus on top of that being the woman of the house.

It kind of makes me happy though that my dad is seeing

Jenni. I know there is a lot of iffy ends with that relationship, but at least I can see my dad smile again. Plus it would be great having another woman around the house. Especially one that i was already close with.

I wonder if I would have to take orders from her if she ever became my step-mother. That would be strange since we are about the same age. She knows me though we use to be best friends so she probably knows I wouldn't listen anyways. I do what I want when I want and no one tells me other wise. My mother and father found that out many times.

There was this one time that they told me I couldn't go out with my friends until my school work was done. Most teenagers would either do the home work or sneak out there window. I however was not an ordinary teenager. I walked right out the front door.

When I got home I got grounded for a month. Even though my sentence only lasted about two days. Like early parole I guess it would be like. It also helps that my I have always had my dad in my pocket. After all I am his only child and on top of that I am his daughter which makes him protect me even more.

My mother and father rarely ever fought, but when they did it was almost always about me. I mean they could have been one of those couples who secretly fought behind closed doors, but if they did they covered their tracks well.

I know my mother would be extremely happy knowing that she has a grandchild on the way. She would not like the idea that I was not married first, but she wouldn't worry to much about it. As long as the baby and I was taken care off. If he was not to take care of me then she would surely cut off his balls. I know one thing though for sure she would spoil the hell out of this child.

I am sitting on the couch right now playing the *PlayStation Four*. My choice of play is *Call of Duty*. Even though since I been pregnant the damn game has aggravated me more than usually. I can normally play for several hours at a time. Now though I am lucky to be able to play an hour without quitting from it getting under my skin so much. My dad always tells me it is just a game calm down. If only he knew why I was like this.

About that time my phone begins to ring. I pause the game and I am annoyed because I am online and know I will still surely die. Probably more than once at that. I think it must finally be my dad, but I am highly disappointed when I see that it is Randy.

Oh now he wants to call. Maybe he realizes his mistake and all he is going to do is say that he is sorry. Blah...Blah...Blah... Been there, heard that before. Men are always the same; they do something wrong and then expect you to just crawl back like we are heartless like them. Sometimes we can get over it, but when you continuously do it of course we are going to get shitty. You might be wonder and if you are you are right. He has done something like this before. After our first date I didn't hear from him for almost a month.

I let the phone go to voice-mail and immediately again he calls. Wow maybe he really is sorry if he calling twice in a row. I probably should let him continue to call for the same amount of days he left me in the dark. So, after five phone calls in a row I finally answer the phone.

"Hello," I snare.

"I been trying to get hold of you."

"I know."

"I probably deserve that considering. I am really sorry."

And the blahs are about to start. I told you this is what would happen. I listen anyways to his boo-hoo story. He states and I quote "*I was crazy minded and that I got scared when you told me the news. I have had time to think about it and I am really glad that you are pregnant.*"

He then continues on asking if I would like to have lunch today and discuss things. Like your typical girl though I accept his offer. Not for me tough, for our child. I want our child to know that his parents will get along no matter what situation for him/her.

I leave the apartment and go to my car. I then drive away from the apartment complex to possibly fix things for our child. I still have one more important thing about this situation to do. This thing is probably going to be the hardest thing too. To tell my father he is going to be a grandfather.

~Chapter 38~

I SLAM DOWN the folder we have on Mr. Brown on my desk in complete frustration. I can not find a damn thing to clear his name. They don't have a lot on him, but they have enough. Especially considering the body was found in the burning car and a lot of evidence with it.

Jenni comes over and massages my shoulders like she has done many times.

"It's going to be okay. We have about five minutes left. We need to make every second count. Don't give up yet," Jenni declares.

"There is no point. We have been over the file a half a dozen times in the past hour. There is nothing. The only thing we don't know is how Frost and Travis are connected," I reply.

"Which could be a good thing after all. If we can't find anything to link them we might be able to save his name after everything is done," she says as she tries to calm me down.

About the time that she says her last word one of the officers in the break room comes out and yells, "The press conference is starting."

Jenni and I stand up and go to the break room. The room is very crowded and we are one of the last ones who entered the room. This is our case though, and we deserve to be on the front row. We push and shove our way to the front. We don't get any troubles because I know that everyone agrees that is how it should be. We finally reach the front and we look directly at the fifty inch flat screen television. I don't know if it is really a fifty inch, but it looks to be the same size as mine.

At the bottom of the screen on *NBC* channel reads this is a special report. We will be back with your original program following the special report. It runs across the screen over and over again.

The program it is interrupting right now at the moment is a newer show on television. Well in a sort of a way it is a new show. The show is called *Family Feud.* That is an old show, but the one that is airing now is is the newer version call *Celebrity Family Feud.*

A few minutes later Captain Green walks outside of the station. Everyone has been so busy we didn't notice that all the press was pulling up outside. That is not where we usually have press conferences, but I guess since it was such an out of the blue moment they had to do what they had to do.

Green swallows his spit and steps up to the microphone. The crowd of the reporters fall silent. Their cameras are all pointing directly at the Captain, like a rifle would when a deer is in its' sights.

"Yesterday there was a car explosion. In that explosion there was a body found. DNA testing has been ran and the name that was associated is Travis Brown. We have found evidence that can not be released at this time that links Mr. Brown to recent murders. So, to be more direct we have reason to believe at this time that Travis Brown is The Chevy Killer," he states to the press.

I feel a tap on my shoulder.

"Not now," I say nicely.

I feel the tap again.

I quickly turn around. "What," I yell.

It is medical examiner, Mr. Jones. He gives me a look like okay calm down asshole.

"What is it?" I change my mood towards him.

"I was looking at Mr. Browns' body and I must ask you a question."

"Go ahead," I answer with a bizarre look upon my face.

"Was your adaptive father an African American by chance?"

"No, he is white. Why?"

"Well, when you examine a body one of the first things you have to do is determine the race of the victims. Well, as you said Mr. Brown is white. When I went to examine your adaptive father I found that the body we have down stairs is African American," Mr. Jones tells me.

"What are you trying to tell me?" I insist.

"That the man down stairs in my examination room is not Travis Brown, your adaptive father," he declares to me.

"Thank you," I tell him.

He nods his head and walks away. I will not humiliate the Captain while he is on television, but I will go to the door and wait for him to come in afterwards. I begin to go do just that when my cell phone rings. The only time is rings is if it is Sarah or Jenni. I know it is not Jenni because she is right beside me. Sarah is not calling either because she set one of those special ring tones. The one that lets me know it is her and no one else. This ring though is a plain old normal ringing.

I take the phone from my pocket and look at the number. The number says that it is a blocked number. If it was a week ago a blocked number would have called me I wouldn't have called it because I didn't know who it was. Last week though, Sarah kept calling blocked and playing pranks. The only reason I found out it was her was because she told me when I got home that day.

I answer the phone by saying, "Yes my darling daughter."

The response I get back though takes my breathe away. The voice on the other side of the line is not that of Sarah's. Instead of Sarah's high pitch woman voice, a low pitch, almost tone death, mans voice answers.

"Wrong detective."

The weird thing though is this voice that answered me sounds familiar.

"Who is this?" I question.

As I respond to him Jenni must have heard me because

she is giving me a strange look. She tries figure out who it is as well, but I just tell her to hold off till I find out myself.

"Come on Mikey you know who this is," the man says.

Michael is my middle name and there is only one person in this world that has every called me by the name Mikey.

"Travis Brown," I declare.

That look that Jenni gave me before only worsens.

"So, you are alive. You need to announce this so we can clear your name."

"I can't do that Mikey. I am not as clear as you might think I am. You need to look back the television," Brown says.

I look up at the television. I see nothing anything different than what we seen before. The Captain is still speaking in front of the press.

"What am I suppose to be looking for?" I yell.

I get no response right away. Well, not a verbal one at least. Seconds later after asking the question I see Captain Green drop to the ground.

I drop the phone and take off running outside where the conference is taking place. I hear screaming coming from the outside. Jenni and I reach her father. She drops to him crying and I feel his pulse, but I stop when I feel nothing. There is a bullet hole in the middle of his forehead.

"He is dead," I say to Jenni.

She begins to cry harder. I stand back to my feet and look around to see possible shooting sights. I don't have to look for long because there is a sign hanging from a building side that reads, *The Chevy Killers are not dead yet.*

Killers this time is what it says. What is that suppose to mean that there is more than one? I put the phone that is still in my hand back up to my ear.

"What the hell are you doing, Travis," I yell.

"What I want to."

"And why did you write killers this time?"

"I have only been the one sniping people. The other victims like the football player and cheerleader. Then the couple under the bridge. There are a few others, but one thing they have in common though is I did not kill them. I can't take credit for work I didn't create," Brown declares over the phone.

"Brown who are the others. I can help you strike a deal, just give me some names," I try to convince him.

"Not going to happen, Mikey."

"Dammit Travis when I find you I am going to put you behind bars for the rest of your life, or worse," I scream.

There is a moment of silence.

"Tell the voices you been hearing in your head I said hello. And oh yeah James game on."

I then hear phone click off on the other side. I put the phone back in my pocket and begin to think. Where have I heard those words before. Then it clicks inside my head. A worried and disgusted look comes on my face.

"What is it?" Jenni asks.

"Frost," I announce, "He is still alive."

~*Chapter 39*~

I RECOGNIZE NOTHING about my surroundings. I am standing in middle of the room as I watch a woman's body is burning up in flames. I can hear the woman screaming out loud calling for help. I don't move though I just stand there and watch as she roasts.

"And how does this make you feel?" Mr. Challenger, my therapist asks.

"When I wake up scared half way to death."

"I don't mean when you wake up. I mean in your dream how do you feel about abandon this mystery woman to her death?" he rewords for me to better understand the question.

Truthfully, I never really thought about it until he asked the question. The way I should feel is bad and ashamed of myself. After all I am a officer of the law and it is in my DNA to protect the innocent. I don't know the woman's back story though so maybe I have a good reason for doing it. That is only part of the dream that takes place. That could be the reason why I don't understand how I could feel nothing.

The worst part about feeling that way is when I do feel about it, I feel some sort of accomplishment flowing throughout my body. As if I am doing what is right in some twisted and sick way.

I tell my doctor, if you consider him a doctor, my thoughts. It is a huge debate whether or not they are truly doctors. In my opinion they are, but that is just my opinion. They help people emotionally and that can sometimes lead to saving their patience lives both physically and mentally.

It is the same debate, in some sort of way, that people argue about whether or not if cheer-leading is a real sport or not. Just to put my statement in there I believe that too is a sport.

My "*doctor*" begins to write some notes down on his piece of paper.

"Will I ever get to know what you write on your papers over there?" I question.

"I just write the main points about our sessions. So when you tell me how you feel or something that is bothering I just make a note of it. It is kind of like when you find some important or interesting information on a case you make sure you make a note of it. It is all the same," Mr. Challenger states.

I am starting to warm up to the man. I have been coming here for about three weeks, with two sessions each week. The first couple of appointments I really didn't say much, but the last few I have really opened up to the doc.

"So, doc you have learned a lot about me. Now, tell me something about you," I insist.

"What would you like to know?" he answers my question with a question.

"I don't know how therapist do it they always do it and quite frantically it gets really annoying. Well, what I am doing right now though is something I like to call building trust. I am taking a step out of the book of the therapist themselves. It is a simple concept actually. All it is really is for you tell something about yourself to get the opposite person to open up more. It helps build a trust factor between doctor and client. I learn this from a movie called *Good Will Hunting*. If you ever get a chance you really should watch it," I state to the doc.

"I have seen it before and you are right it is a very good movie. You still did not answer the question though. What is it you would like to know about me detective."

"Oh, but I did answer you, sir. See by saying that I was stating that I am willing to learn anything about you. That it didn't matter what you told me. However though you did answer the question without knowing it. See now i know that you like watching movies," I laugh.

"Ah you think you beat me at this game, but you didn't.

Yes, I said I liked that movie. I however did not say I enjoy watching several other movies. In fact, the only reason I watched the movie was because I watched it while I was in school to get my therapy license. I had no choice, but to watch it. In reality I barely watch any kind of television at all. As you may know people with our kinds of professions find it hard to have spare time," he directs to me as he just landed his death blow in a war.

He does have a very good point though about not having time to do much of anything beside work. My daughter and I are decently close, but not as close as we should be. If we were I would have been told already were she goes at night. She is twenty-one though and will tell me some day I guess.

"You win then doc. I guess the question would be something simple then. Do you have a family?"

"I did before. Unfortunately, they were murdered by Scott Frost."

I feel my nerves tighten as that name comes out to my ears. it is as if someone has poured boiling water in my ears it hurt so bad to hear that name.

"I heard on the news that he was murdered himself by you to be exact."

I sit and wonder were he is about to go with this.

"When I seen you on my client list I couldn't wait to meet you and thank you for what you did to that man. So, thank you for doing the right thing for both of our families sake," Challenger states.

I want to say you're welcome, but I can't. Not after everything that I had learned about him still possibly being alive. I just nod my head to tell him that he was welcome. It was the only professional way I knew how to do it.

I look up at the clock to break the awkwardness that is surrounding the room now.

"Hey look at that. Time is up for the day."

I stand up and shake the therapists hand and begin to walk out of the room. I walk out and get in my car. As I start up my engine I have a thought that is now troubling me. As I have said before I have been in the department since the first murders of Frost. I know every victims name and that now includes all of the victims from The Chevy Killer as well.

The point I am trying to get at is that none of the victims go by the name of Mrs. Challenger. Even if they went by another name I would have remembered Mr. Challengers' face. Like I said though that is the problem I don't remember nothing about the case he is talking about. So, if his family wasn't killed by Frost why is he saying that they were?

~Chapter 40~

I REACH MY destination at a little Italian restaurant. That is where I am suppose to meet Randy at for lunch. Like I said before I am only doing this for our unborn child. I am tired of dealing with his bull shit and I will not put my self in a situation where a man treats me like I am dirt again.

That being said, no matter how bad he did me wrong I will not keep him from his child.

The restaurant is an outdoor one. Now that it is spring time it is perfect time to come out and enjoy the weather. That is when it is not raining these days. I walk up to the waiter and say that I am here with someone.

Moments later a shaggy, dirty blonde, headed man approaches me. The man is about six foot and has bulky built to him. Which makes sense considering the man plays semi-pro football for one of the teams up here. He is about twenty-eight and is very handsome at that. I know all of this because the man that is approaching me is Randy.

"Hey dear." He states as he reaches in to kiss my cheek. I stick out my cheek for him just to be polite of course. I am trying to have friendly conversation and I don't want to be rude right off the bat.

We find our seat right by the fence that separates us from the people who are walking on the sidewalk. I try not to stare at the people who pass even though they are looking at us eating. It really makes me feel uncomfortable. Especially since I am now pregnant and feel like I eat like a cow.

"What did you want to talk about?" I question out of

moments of silence.

"Just about everything going on. The child your carrying and us," he declares.

Of course he wants to talk about that.

"Let me say this first without being rude Randy. You can be there for our child, but as far as us it will not happen."

"Oh okay," he states.

He had one hand in his pocket and the other hand on the table. The hand on the table is sweating like crazy and he removes the other hand from his pocket when I tell him there will be no us.

"Do you have something in your pocket?"

"What?" he asks.

"You removed your hand from you pocket when I said that. It was as if you were about to pull out something," I say.

"Oh it doesn't matter."

"It does to, show it to me," I insist.

He thinks about it for a minute and then I guess decides to show me. He puts his hand back in his pocket and pulls it back out. When he does there is a black box he is holding. He opens it and when he does there is a gorgeous diamond ring. My jaw drops to the concrete floor I am so shocked.

"I have had a lot of time to think about us in the past couple weeks. It is part of the reason I didn't call or try to see you so that I could be sure. So, what do you say?" he blurts out.

I hesitated in my decision because when I first came to meet him I knew nothing about us would ever happen again. Now though he is popping out a ring on me and asking me to marry him. How much more serious could it get? That is what I was worried about this whole time was he didn't care, but this obviously says different.

"I just need a little time to think about it, okay?"

He frowns and replies, "I completely understand."

"I know one thing though if you really want me to think about this then you will never ran away again like you did," I announce.

He agrees with me and I can tell he has hope in his eyes. I get up from my chair because I need to leave.

"I have to go. I want to see you tonight though."

"Well, where are you going?" he asks.

"I have to go tell my father about something," I smile.

I walk over and give him a kiss on his cheek. I then leave the restaurant and go towards my car. When I reach my door I go to open it, but I am startled by a man that just approached me.

He is dressed in a nice suit. I know nothing really about clothes so I can't give you the brand, but I can tell it is expensive.

"Oh shit, you scared me."

"I am sorry. I didn't mean to," the man says.

"What can I do for you?"

"I am special agent Bruce Jackson with the FBI. You should be careful," he states.

He then hands me a card and then walks away. I study the card for a second, but then look up again. I catch the FBI agent before he is to far away.

"What is this?"

"If you ever find out anything weird going on you should give me a call. Your boyfriend is not who he says he is," the agent yells back.

He then disappears in the crowd of people. As he does so I look over to where Randy is still sitting at the table. Every trust he has gained in the past hour is now in question because of what the FBI agent just said.

~Chapter 41~

IT HAS BEEN a few weeks since the death of our late Captain Green. Not only has it put a strain on everyone at work, but one at home just as well.

I lost a very good friend, probably my best friend. My girlfriend lost her father. Which is doing nothing good for my relationship at all right now.

So, if you had been wondering how my days has been please don't ask or even think about it because it has been a horrible damn day. Just like the last couple of weeks.

Jenni hasn't left the station since. She is trying to dig up any possible lead that we might have, but everything ends up turning towards a dead end. She is the way I was when I first lost my wife. She is determined to find justice for the son-of-a-bitch who did this.

The good thing though is that we at least know who committed the murder we just have to find him and whatever accomplishes he may have, if any. I say if any because, Travis Brown might have been just trying to get us off his trail. He could have possibly be making us look at ghost. That is not the case though we have hired extra help and most of our resources are in on this.

Most of the time local PD and the FBI do not play along well, but as you can tell this is not most the time. We must do what we have to in order to bring justice to the one(s) responsible for these crimes.

    I walk in with my shoulders slouched over and my head lowered. I think I speak for everyone when I say everyday that passes is another day we take a step towards failure. It doesn't help that the killers went from killing weekly to now at random. Well, it is a good thing because they aren't killing more people. I felt that I should have to rephrase that because it just sounded wrong to me. The only bad part is though we never know when or who they will strike next or how.

    "Hey darling. I bring gifts," I say to Jenni as I walk to her over by her desk.

    In my hand I have a bag from *Taco Bell*. Jenni absolutely loves their breakfast. It doesn't matter what it is just as long as it is from there.

    She cracks a little smile at me. The closest I seen to one in weeks. We are making progress at least I say internally. I go over grab my chair and bring it to her desk.

    "You have any luck yet?"

    "No not yet. I however did get the information you asked for finally," she redirects.

    "Which one? The labs are slow," I laugh.

    She laughs as well she pulls out a piece of paper. I just felt like I won the the championship of boxing because I made her laugh finally.

    She hands me the paper and I look at it. It is the paper stating the ownership of the island.

    "Just as I thought," I mumble.

    Even though I said it softly Jenni heard what I said.

    "What do you mean?" she questions.

    "When that lab came back saying my fingerprints were all over that paper that Travis Brown threw away after killing Mrs. James I started looking around. I didn't find anything to back my theory until now." I announce.

    "Oh what may that theory be?"

    "I believe that Frost and Brown are setting me up to take the fall for everything."

~*Chapter 42*~

JENNI BEGINS TO laugh out loud so hard her face turns red. I don't get what is so funny about this. Maybe she had a funny thought race through her mind and she is finally letting out anything and everything inside out.

"Did I say something funny?" I laugh with her.

"You really think they would go through all that trouble just to frame you, James?"

"How else do you explain that my fingerprints got on that paper? That the island I was kidnapped and placed on is somehow magically under my name? Brown is close to me. I mean after all he knows every personal thing about me. From my social security number to my bank accounts. He has easy access to anything of mine he wants. It makes perfect sense," I proclaim.

Jenni stops laughing. I am guessing because it is starting to make sense of it all as well.

"There is still just one thing I really don't get out of any of this."

"What may that be?"

"How in the hell is Frost still alive? You said you chopped off his damn head," she interrogates.

"I am really not sure about that, but it is something I need to find out. That and how Frost and Brown are connected. There are always a connection dear. You just have to find the right ones. When we do we will surely find the other killers as well," I say proudly.

She smiles a fake smirk my way. We continue to discuss

things about the case for about half an hour when a elder man walks through the door of the second floor. Everyone in this building and possibly this city knows who this man is. It is Commissioner Alex Book.

The Commissioner has been in his chair for longer than I can recall at this moment. He only makes trips down here when there is something important to be told.

"I need to see detective Gibbs up on the third floor immediately," he echos and then limps out of room.

The limp is from a car crash he had several years back. I have heard rumors surrounding him saying he is going have to give up his chair within the next couple years.

Once the man walks out everyone's attention turns towards me and only me. That definitely includes all of Jenni's attention. Which is something I have not had since her fathers death.

"What is going on?" I see her lip the words to me quietly.

I shrugg my shoulders and tell her to come along with me to find out. She gives me a dirty look and tells me that there is no way in hell she would do that without the Commissioners permission. I grunt as I walk past her and out of the room.

~Chapter 43~

I WALK UP the stairway to the third floor just as the Commissioner asked. Well, more like commanded. He too is ex-military and he has no problem barking orders at anyone.

David once told me a story about how they were in a meeting with the Mayor and the Commissioner brought the Mayor down a few levels. A very intimidating man if you ask me, but I have never been scared of anyone. So, don't ask me to start now because it won't happen.

I reach the third floor and walk into an unfamiliar territory. Tara desk had been empty, but everyone in the station already knew that one. When David was shot and killed Tara found it to hard to stick around and put in her resignation a few days later.

The floor seemed so plain without anyone up her. The only people who have been up here since the unexpected turn of events was maintenance to fix a leak from the rain.

I walk into the once David Green's office. There the Commissioner sat behind the desk.

"Good morning , Commissioner," I state.

"Detective Gibbs," he answers as he stands up to shake my hand.

"I am deeply sorry for your loss. I know that David and you were close friends and partners. I can't imagine how it must feel to lose someone like that," he continued.

He really couldn't imagine it because it is a pain you can only feel when it has happen to you. Even then though everyone acts differently to losing people. Some can handle their emotions other just absolutely lose it and go off the deep end. So far I am one of the first type.

"Thank you sir," is what I reply to him though.

"How is your family doing?" he asks.

"We are doing good. My daughter and I are having dinner tonight to discuss something important she says. I never really did agree to it, but I was left without a choice. You know how it is with daughters."

In fact yes he did know considering he has five daughters.

"Yes, I sure do," he laughs.

"Well, not to be disrespectful, sir, but I have tons of work to do. So, what is this all about?" I ask as nicely as possible.

"Tell your daughter," is all I hear at first.

Did I or did I not just tell him I was extremely busy with my case. This is why I hate when people from higher up come in. They once worked our jobs you would think they would understand how hard and how much time we need.

He continues on his sentence though and I feel bad.

"You can tell your daughter that you will be eating out at fancy restaurant tonight. Congratulations, Gibbs you have just been promoted to Captain. If you choice to accept the position."

I nearly choke on my spit when he says this to me. It takes me a good minute or two, probably closer to five minutes before I soak in what the Commissioner just said.

"Are you serious?" I ask.

"Yes, the Mayor gave me the call this morning to come tell you."

I can not help, but to smile from ear to ear. The second thing that crosses my mind though is David and how happy he would have been for me if he was here. The third thing though that pops into my head is the best part of it all. If I was to take this promotion then I could be the one who brought down the killers who killed our former Captain.

"I accept on one condition," I announce.

"Yes?"

"I would like for myself to be allowed to continue to be a detective as well. For me to be out there in the field and doing crime scenes as well. As I am sure you know the men in war follow their commanding officers that would go to battle with them, not the one who would hide behind a desk in Washington."

"I will pass it along to the Mayor and see what he thinks. I am sure he will say this is fine. He likes it when one of his team members has the balls to do something like this. So, as long as the Mayor accepts it then come tomorrow you will be the new Captain of CPD." the commissioner states.

I really like the sound of that Captain Gibbs. It has a nice ring to if I may say.

~*Chapter 44*~

SARAH AND I enter the apartment. She has decided that she wanted to make dinner tonight rather than go out to a fancy restaurant. She said that I might not feel like driving after the fact.

I rather have a home cook meal from her anyways. She gets her good cooking from her mother. It definitely did not come from me. I probably couldn't even cook a thing of noodles. That is why I eat out most of the time. That would also be the reason for me gaining a belly over the last couple of years.

Sarah is making this delicious dish that her mother first made called, *Cheesy Chicken Spaghetti.* My wife just made the original meal, but my daughter has tweaked it by adding, trading, and removing things until the point the dish is perfection for my taste. We haven't had this in a very long time and here lately I have been craving the hell out of it. I never been pregnant nor do I ever intend on that happening so I can't say this for sure. The way though, that I've been craving it lately is like a woman craving their own unique dish while they are pregnant.

"How much longer?" I ask from the couch.

We had decided that we would watch a movie in the process. She wanted to watch something on *Netflix*, but I wanted to watch *Star Wars* series. We finally compromised as we agreed to watch something from *Netflix* before and during supper. Then after dinner and the "important topic" we would watch *Star Wars*.

I still have not the slightest idea about what it is she needs to talk about. I don't let it bother me either because like I have said many times before she will tell me when she is ready.

She gets up from the couch and goes to check the timer.

"About ten minutes," she states.

"Thank the Lord. The smell of it is killing me on the wait," I laugh.

Sarah comes back to the living room and gives me a kiss on my cheek. She then hands me a beer from the fridge. Yes, I have picked up the habit again. I had quit for the longest time, but I guess everything has gotten to me lately. I don't drink a bunch just enough to calm my nerves. Sarah doesn't worry about it because she knows I am a lot of more mature than I use to be about the subject.

A few minutes later the door bell rings. I give Sarah a look like who is that. She just smiles at me.

"It's okay, I invited a couple of people."

"Oh okay," I state confusedly.

That would explain why she made a whole lot of extra.

I watch as she goes over to the door and open it. In walks Jenni a milli-second later. I try to hide my beer quickly because I didn't tell her yet that I was starting again, not that she would be mad about me doing it anyways. She might be pissed though that I didn't tell her.

Jenni walks into the room and gives me a kiss on my lips.

"I invited her. I think since you guys are together she should have to hear this as well. That and she is still my best friend," Sarah smiles.

Not even five minutes later the door bell rings again. Sarah once again goes and answers it. When she answers the door this time though I don't recognize the person at all. Now I am starting to worry just a bit because the person standing in the doorway is a man.

I swallow my pride and get up from the couch. I walk over to my daughter and the mystery man.

"Randy this is my dad. Dad this is Randy, my finance," she announces.

Her what I yell inside. Why in the hell did I not know

anything about this? I keep calm though probably because the beer I had helped.

"Nice to meet you sir," Randy states.

"You as well," I respond as I give Sarah a death glare. "Anymore surprises?"

"Not like that. He just purposed this morning," she tries to explain.

By now I am over the whole situation. At least I know where she has been when she says she is staying at the office.

I tell him to come in and to have a seat in the living room since that is where we will be eating. We both talk about some things as Jenni and Sarah prepare the plates.

He doesn't seem to be that bad then again that is probably the way most are. He does have a good paying job though. He says he works for my daughters company which is probably how they met.

Before they bring us the plates he asks where the bathroom is. I tell him being polite. As soon as he leaves the room I turn around to face Sarah. She lips the words, "I am sorry."

I then see Jenni lip wording something as well. "Drop it and let it be," she says.

I turn back around to face the television. When I do I notice that Randy's wallet had fell out of his pocket. I quickly grab and look for some information. his drivers license says Randy Rogers and so does his Social Security Number. There is another piece of paper though that has a different name on it. It reads, *Josh Myers.*

I hear Randy, or whoever he is flush the toilet. I don't have much time to continue to spy. I quickly write both his names and Social Security Number down.

I am caught in the process of putting the wallet back. Not by Randy though it is by Jenni.

"I said drop it," she whispers angrily in my ear.

"Fine!" I exclaim back.

Randy then enters back into the room and just in time for the plates to reach us. We then proceed to eat and watch the movie on the television. The movie we are watching is really kind of stupid. I agreed to it though.

"The movie after this won't be as boring. We are going to get to watch *Star Wars*," I laugh.

Everyone seemed to enjoy the idea of that, everyone, but Sarah of course. I can't wait for the new one to come out later this year.

I finish my plate and take it to the sink in the kitchen. About that time my phone rings. I look at it and it is the station. I ignore it the first time, but then Jenni phone begins to ring. Which can not be a good thing if both of our phones are going on.

"I will call them," I tell her.

I do just and it rings a couple times before anyone answers. Finally, they pick up the phone.

"This is detective Gibbs."

It is another one of the detectives at the station that is on the phone.

"There is a Mr. Challenger that says he needs to speak with you sir."

"Ask him if it can wait until the morning. I am having a very important family dinner tonight," I try.

I hear the detective ask Mr. Challenger, but I don't hear the therapist. A few seconds later the detectives comes back on the phone.

"Sir, he insist that he must talk to you now. He says that it is very important that he speaks with you immediately," the detective states.

I grunt and I must have been heard from the detective.

"Would you like me to make sure he doesn't come back until the morning. I must say he looks pretty frighten right now," the detective adds.

"No, that is fine. Tell him that I will be there as soon as possible," I answer as I hang up the phone.

"Is everything okay?" Sarah asks.

"Nothing to big. I have to go down to the station there is a man who needs to speak with me is all. It shouldn't take very long at all. An hour or two at most," I announce.

Jenni grabs her coat and joins me.

"Must you go to?" Sarah asks Jenni.

"Yeah. It will give you some time alone with Randy."

Jenni winks.

I give Jenni a nudge on the shoulder to tell her really you didn't just say that. I know that my daughter is old enough to be doing stuff, but she is still my daughter and I don't want her to be doing it. just as any other father would. Jenni and Sarah just laugh.

We go to try to leave once again. We once again are stopped by Sarah's voice.

"Dad!" she yells.

"Yes, honey."

"I need to tell you something," she states.

"Can it not wait till I get back?" I question.

"Not really because I don't know when I will be able to build up the courage to say it again," she struggles to say.

I walk over to her and give her a kiss.

"You have all the courage in the world, honey. I know you can wait till later. It will only be a couple hours," I politely state.

I walk away again.

"Dad, I am pregnant," she screams at me.

I stop in the hallway and turn back to her. I can tell from the facial expression she is straight up serious. I then do something I shouldn't I storm out of the apartment and slam the door behind me.

~Chapter 45~

I HIT THE acceleration gas pedal as I storm through traffic. I have my sirens on because I want to hurry up and get to the station and get this over with. Then I am going home and Mr. Rodgers better hope he is not there.

"Honey, slow down please you are starting to scare me," Jenni tries to reason with me.

I say nothing, but I do slow down a bit so that I wouldn't scare her as much.

"This is bull shit. She is only nineteen and has her entire life ahead of her. The last thing she needs right now is a baby on the way. She is way to young," I exclaim.

"I know, but what has happened has already taken place there is nothing you can do now."

I just grunt and roll my eyes. I then dig in my pockets and find the piece of paper that I wrote Randy's information on. I hand it to Jenni.

"First thing in the morning I need you to look up some information on my daughters boyfriend," I declare.

"James Michael Gibbs, please tell me you did not go detective mode on your daughters baby daddy."

"What? It is a father thing. Just please do it. I find some cards and papers in his wallet under a different name. I just want to make sure he is who he is says he is," I insist towards her.

"Fine," she replies even though I know she still doesn't want to.

"Wait why can't you do it yourself?" she questions.

"I will be moving us and our things in our new office." I

state.

"Our new office?"

"I am taken over your fathers position. You will be joining me though because I am still being a detective. The mayor has already approved it. So, we both will be moving up there."

She kisses me on my cheek, "That is so great."

I know that it will bother her a little bit knowing that is the room her father use to work in. I am glad though she is happy for me. By me having that chair I will be able to do more good for this town especially with Jenni by my side.

About that time we pull into the station.

I walk in and go to the second level where my desk is. I would sit down in my chair like usual, but I can't because someone else is sitting in my chair. To be exact it is Mr. Challenger sitting in my chair.

Jenni and I walk up to him. I introduce the two of them and then get straight down to business.

"Not to be rude, but I was having a family important family meal this better be something good," I state to therapist.

"You remember that dream you told me about the other day?"

"Yeah of course," I answer.

"Well, I got home and began to think about things you said. The house and lady you describe lives right next door to me. Last night there was a fire there."

"That is a matter that has to deal with the fire department, not the police department," I state.

"That might be true, but I am sure that your station as been notified of the findings inside that house."

"Not that I can think of at the moment."

"The firemen found my neighbor in the house dead. They also said that the body was chopped into separate pieces. Which if I remember right is a matter for the police department," the therapist insist.

~Chapter 46~

I TAKE MR. Challenger to interrogation room one just to get his statement on everything. I put it on camera and then I thank him for the information. I tell him we will look into it first thing in the morning. Jenni and I then proceed to go back to my apartment.

Jenni tries to plead with me to not do anything stupid when we get home. I don't exactly give her a yes or no answer any of the times that she states the comment to me.

We reach the apartment and go straight in. When I walk in and the entire place is dark except for the television that is on in the living room.

We walk into the room and see that Randy and Sarah are asleep on the couch together. At first I am angry at the sight. That all goes away though when I see the smile upon my daughters face while she is asleep.

This guy must really make her happy in whatever way possible. I bend down and wake the two of them from the couch. I see Sarah slowly open and the same goes for Randy. Sarah is surprised to see me, but Randy's facial expression is terrified.

"I would like to talk to the both of you," I say calmly.

They follow me to our kitchen table. At one end they sit and at the other end is Jenni and I. Both sets of couples are holding hands to comfort one another. I think about how what and how I am going to say some things. Then I begin.

"First off I want to say congratulations on your big news."

"Thank you," they respond.

I hold up my and as they do so to tell them to stop.

"Just wait until I finish saying everything," I state.

They sit back in their chairs all the way and prepare for my speech.

"I also want to say that I am sorry for the way I acted when I found out. With that being said you have to understand why I did. As of yesterday I had no knowledge of you having a boyfriend, Sarah, let alone you were getting married. Then you proceed to tell me that you guys are having a baby together. It is a lot to take in," I say.

"I know and..." Sarah says.

"I am not quite finished yet," I pause and then continue on, "You have to think you are only nineteen years old dear. Randy you look young yourself, but with that being said I know age is a number. I can speak for my daughter when I say that I know she is mature enough to have this baby. I am sorry I can't say that for you yet Randy, but that is because I just met you. What I am getting at though is I don't want you guys getting married for the wrong reasons and I would really appreciate it if you guys take a little more time to think about this huge decision. That is all that I ask from you guys."

My daughter smiles and walks over gives me a huge kiss on the cheek. I give her one back and I stand up to hold my precious baby in my arms like I did when she was first born.

"Do we know if it is a boy or a girl yet?" I question.

"Not yet. We are suppose to find out next week though. I promise that you will find out when we know." Sarah insist.

"Well I have a couple more days of PTO (Pay time off for those who are not in the work force yet.), and I would love to be a the doctor when you find out," I smile.

"Of course," she states.

I go over and shake Randy's hand and ask for a word with him. He agrees right away as we tell the girls we will be right back.

One good thing about this apartment is that I have a outdoor balcony. That is where Randy and I are heading towards right now.

I open the door and we walk out. The moon is full and

their is not a cloud in sight meaning we can see all the stars visible to the human eye. It is a mild, not muggy temperature outside.

I close the door and make sure the girls are no where near the door. Well, mainly just Sarah because Jenni already knows why I am pulling him out here. When I make sure she is no where close enough to hear I begin to speak with Randy.

"Once again congratulations," I state as I pull out two cigars out of my pocket one for each of us. They are the same brand that David and I smoked before in his office. I gained the possession of the cigars the same exact way that David did as well. I got them as a gift from the Mayor, for getting the Captain chair.

I pull out a lighter as well and light the both our cigars.

"Once again congratulations on the baby," I say to start off the conversation.

"Thank you," he responds.

"A lot of things change when you have a child. You will protect them at all cost, especially if your child is a girl. Between that and my detective skills I hate that I am even bringing this up. With that being said though I must protect my daughter from any possible harm," I take a deep breathe and then continue on, "Earlier tonight when you asked where the bathroom was you dropped your wallet. When you went to the bathroom I peaked into it. Like I said before it is the detective side of me. I couldn't help, but to notice the two different names you had on things. I am not hear to arrest you or even care about what it is you are doing. I am just here to say don't bring my daughter into it or hurt her and we will be fine. If you do either one of those things I will find you and I will kill you."

I can see him swallow the smoke from the cigar. After coughing on the smoke he begins to laugh. I feel kind of offended that he is laughing at me. I know many people who think I am a scary person and this guy is just laughing at the image of me at my worse.

"I am sorry. Did I say something funny?" I interrogate.

"Yeah," he answers unexpectedly.

This boy has some serious balls. We are on the tenth

floor of this apartment complex. I wonder if he would still be laughing if I push his disrespectful ass off the edge.

Then I would have to deal with the station and even worse Sarah. I could always say he was not use to the buzz from the cigar and tripped. I tried to save him, but he was to far away. Sounds like a pretty good plan to me.

"You must be talking about the Josh Myers name, right?" he states.

"Yeah."

"That is my cousin. He always loses his wallet and he asked me to keep his important papers safe for him."

Well, now I feel like a total ass. I should have known that there was some reasonable answer for it. I just let my detective instincts get the best of me.

"I am sorry. I know I must look like a hard ass," I tell him.

"It is okay you are just protecting your child like you said. I completely understand," Randy answers.

"How about we pretend this night didn't happen? How about we start off fresh?" I try to convince him.

"Sounds good to me," he replies as he sticks out his hand to shake mine.

~Chapter 47~

I WALK INTO the station and stay on the first floor. When my father was alive I would either go to see him or I would go to my desk on the second floor (Now on the third floor.). Today, though I am going to the computer lab we have so I can do some research on Randy Rodgers.

James told me last night when we went to bed last night to not to do it anymore, but I believe he was letting his emotions get the best of him last night. Plus last time he told me to do something I took forever to do it and in a way it could have helped my father live. So, this time when he asked me to do something I am still going to carry it out and this time immediately.

I try to sneak my way in there the same way that a teenager would sneak back into the house in the middle of the night. I don't even know why I am sneaking we detectives have all the access we want to the computer lab. I feel like I am in a *Mission Impossible* movie, and I am on a secret mission.

I enter the room and go to the very back computer in a corner. There is only one other person in the room and that is another detective that I just know of. He has helped James several times he said, but I like to just stick to my partner. It is the best way not to run into any corrupt cops.

I log in my user ID and my password. I change my password almost every other week that away there is no way that anyone can figure it out. There only person who knows when it changes and what it is when I do change it is James.

Finally , I get the database screen pop up. I immediately

typed in Randy Rodgers and all the information needed to find his identity. It takes a second for the information to come to the screen.

It says he is twenty-one. That he was born in Miami, Florida. It continues on with a bunch more useless information. I reach the bottom and nothing suspicious pops up. As far as I can tell Randy Rodgers is as clean as a person who has OCD.

I exit his name out and about to give up when I have a thought. I go to put in the second name that James gave me to just see if what Randy told James was the truth.

I type in Josh Myers along with the same information I entered for Randy. When I do it does not take long before the red flags start flying.

The picture of Randy's so called cousin looks identical to Randy. I look down the list and most of the information is the same as well. However though, Josh Myers has a past. He is wanted in Florida questioning in connection to a murder of a high school girl five years ago.

That is not all though, the list continues on with four more names. One each year and all on the same date, March 23rd. that date is only ten days away. I continue to read on about the information. He is just wanted for questioning for all five murders. he is not a suspect according to the records, but he has to be if he is wanted that many times. it says that he disappeared the same day the women died every single time.

There was the lady in Florida, then there other four bodies left a pattern going due North. They were located in Georgia, Tennessee, Kentucky, and Indiana. Now he is here in Illinois and is dating my best friend.

Now who do I tell Sarah who can just get away from the man? Or do I tell James? If I do tell James he could have him arrested and possibly convicted. I know how James is though, he is so protective over his daughter. If he finds out this piece of information he will either beat Randy so bad he will want to die, or James will just kill him.

Whatever I decide to do though I must do it fast because if he is the one murdering these women then my best friend only has ten days left before she becomes his next victim.

~Chapter 48~

I RUSH TO MY car and speed off towards James and Sarah's apartment. Even though it is both of theirs apartment I am only going to see one this time, Sarah.

To get out of the station without being questioned from James about where I was going I had to lie. I couldn't tell him my real destination and the reasoning behind it. He would completely lose it. I used the one about how I have to sort some things out with my dads' will. He is always very caring when it comes to the subject of my father. More now after his death than he did before. So, as bad as this may sound, I use this to my advantage.

The entire way to the apartment I constantly call Sarah's phone to warn her I would be there soon. Every time though I am left with disappointment as I get the same results; no answer and straight to voicemail. I continue to call anyways though, hoping that I get lucky.

I reach the street of their apartment. It normally takes me about twenty to thirty minutes to get there from the station when my shift ends, not today though. it only takes me ten to fifteen minutes.

When I reach the apartment I am suppose to park in the garage across the street. This however, doesn't happen. I instead park on the curb that is located in front of the apartment complex.

I do this because I don't have time to waste. I still haven't figured out his kill tactics. I don't know whether or not if he likes to do his killing on the spot. Or is he a psychopath and enjoy the hunt of the game. That he starts off by kidnapping them days before. I go to the elevator and wait as it seems like it takes forever to reach me. I finally, get tired of waiting even though I only wait for thirty seconds. Thirty seconds to long in my books. I dart for the stairway. I know exactly where the stairway is because I have to take them every time that I walk up with James. Some stupid thing about he likes the stairway better. Even though, lately he has taken the elevator a few dozen more times.

    I take all ten levels worth of steps. I approach the apartment door. As I do so I pull out the key that James gave me about two months ago. I think I should knock first because I don't want to startle anyone anymore than I already have.

    Just as I raise my fist to pound on the door I hear a roar of Sarah screaming and something break from inside the apartment. My first initial thought is that he is doing it right at this moment and that I am going to catch him in the act.

    I slowly, but quickly insert my key into the keyhole. I turn the lock as quietly as possible. As I open the door I pull out my pistol from my hostler. I creep through the hallway and to the edge of a corner.

    Sarah is still making the noises. I follow the noises to the living room. When I am close enough I jump out and yell, "Freeze, and put your hands in the air,"

    I want to add mother fucker to the end of it. To bad I couldn't do my best impression of Samuel L. Jackson right now. It would be just the perfect time for it. I instead just keep it the normal warning rather than a insulating one.

    When I come around the corner I see Sarah's big bouncing breast come to a stop. She quickly covers them quickly from my view with her hands. It is not like I haven't seen them before considering she is my best friend. Awkward I know, but the truth.

    "Jenni, what the hell?" she yells.

    "I thought..." I start to say then think about the next words about to come out of my mouth. I change my approach, "I really need to talk to you."

"Can it wait? I am sort of in the middle of something right now." she asks.

Before I can answer Randy butts into the conversation, "It's okay I am late for work anyways. That is one good thing about dating the boss," he laughs as he stands up from the couch.

I can understand why Sarah is so attract to him. He has a very nice athletic body tone and what appears to be smooth skin. If I was not with James I would definitely take a hit at him if Sarah hadn't. Well, that is until I found out he was a psychotic murdering son-of-a-bitch.

I step to the kitchen to turn my back as they get dressed. I feel like I am a mother who just walked in on their child having sex. That is in a way exactly what just happened. I can't really call Sarah my daughter though considering we are basically the same age.

Randy gives Sarah a kiss as he begins to leave. There is something about the look he gives me as he walks by me. It's like he is really pissed off because I stopped him from abducting my best friend. As soon as he closes the door Sarah darts my way and she is pissed off.

"What in the hell was that all about? Coming in and telling my finance to put up his hands and shit?"

"I thought something bad was happening in here," I try to sound convincing.

"What did you think was happening?" she questions.

"That doesn't matter. What does matter is that you need to listen to what I am about to tell you. Randy is not who he says he is. His real name is Josh Myers and is not that nice guy I met the other night," I carry on.

"You ran a background on him. Are you serious?"

"Yes, and I was nervous at first to do it. What I found out about him though, makes me happy that I did," I announce back to her, like a mother getting onto her teenager.

She pauses for a minute and then starts to carry on again, "Did my father put you up to this? I swear if he did."

"No, your father had no knowledge of this. I was looking out for my best friend is all. I went about it all wrong as I let my detective instinct take over. Dammit though Sarah it was worth it. You really need to just stop and listen to what I have to say," I declare.

"No. If my father has no knowledge of this then keep it that way. I have this situation under control. We are going on a mini-vacation to celebrate our engagement. We will be back in about a weeks time," Sarah states.

"Please, Sarah don't do this. I am begging you."

"It is to late we are about to leave this afternoon. Give my father my loves."

She then walks out of the apartment. It is not longer after I do the same. When I reach the spot where my car was parked I notice that it is no longer there. I take a glance down the road and see it being towed off.

"I knew I should have parked that damn thing in the parking garage," I argue with myself.

I stop to think about how Sarah acted in the apartment when I tried to tell her the news. It was almost as if she already knew about it, but how? She said she had the situation under control. So, I guess the better question would be what is she planning to do about it?

I pick up the phone and begin to dial James' phone number. I have to now even if ever nerve in my body is telling me not to. Sarah is forcing my hand. So, in return I will force hers back. She might be severely ticked off at me, but at least she would still be alive to do so.

~Chapter 49~

I OPEN THE DOOR to the Lincoln TownCar and I sit right into the passengers seat. Special Agent Bruce Jackson is in the drivers seat beside me.

"Who was the woman?" he questions.

"A friend who found out about Randy's true past."

"Maybe you should let her in on the mission. That way she can give you extra protection."

"No!" I exclaim. "We must do this on our own."

"Yes, but there is no sure way of promising I can protect you and your unborn baby if you go through with this," he insists.

"I know what I was signing on to. After all I am the one who brought this to your attention. And besides I would be in so much more danger if I hadn't came to you guys. You are the FBI I am sure you guys can protect me better than my friend," I declare.

"Very well," he gives up.

He turns on the car and we begin to drive off down the road. I reach in my pocket and grab my cell phone. Then I proceed to dial a number.

"What are you doing?" Bruce questions.

"Calling a tow truck for my friends car."

"A little bit extreme don't you think?"

"If you knew my friend then you would know that she would follow us. It is for her own good that I do this. It will keep her out of harm herself," I state.

He says nothing back to me in response. Instead he drives directly top the FBI Headquarters for Chicago. The station is much bigger than the one I am use to seeing. My father's station is a pretty good size, but it has to considering it is the Chicago Police Department. The headquarters for the FBI though puts my father's station to complete shame.

It is much cleaner and very high tech compared to the normal police station. If you were driving down the road and not paying attention it would be easy to pass it and never notice it. It might be a big building and all, but it blinds in with all the other company buildings downtown.

It is made of glass on all sides which is weird for me because you would think they would want to keep everything confidential in that place. To be honest, the only reason I know it is their station is because, I see a huge sign at reads Federal Bureau of Investigations of the Chicago Division on one side.

Like I said though, if you weren't paying attention you wouldn't have noticed it. I was paying attention and nearly missed it myself.

"Just remember what we discussed about," Bruce says.

"I will," I respond.

"If we play this mission out right then in about a weeks time from now we will have the fugitive known as Josh Myers will be in FBI custody," the agent states.

~Chapter 50~

I WALK DOWN TO the medical examiners office. Which should be really fun considering I just dumped a random body on his table. To make it even worse it was random and not technically part of our case. Well, to be exact it arrived here about three this morning. I also should quit saying a body because all that is left of this person I sent Mr. Jones is the persons' bones.

The bones were separated, but Mr. Jones was able to piece them back together to make it look at least human like again. On one of the toes of the bones is a tag that reads Abbe McDonald, who just so happens to be Mr. Challenger's former neighbor.

I couldn't help, but to be drawn to this case. After all I did dream, or had a vision, whichever you want to call it, this murder. It hasn't officially been labeled a homicide yet. Hopefully, the information that Mr. Jones is about to give me though will confirm it.

"Hello, Jones," I says as I walk through the door.

"Captain."

"Non-sense. It is still James or Gibbs."

"Fine, Captain Gibbs."

Smartass I think to myself.

"So, what did you find out about the body I shipped to you?" I question.

"Thank you for the early morning wake up call, by the way. I might have been pissed off a little bit if I was asleep, but I wasn't. I had a visit from one of my smoking hot Russian friend. I am still curious though why we are working on a case that is out of our jurisdiction?" He answers me with a question.

"Because I said so. Now what is it you found?"

He salutes me in another smartass way. Then he symbols for me to follow him. I do just as he asks as we enter the actual examination room. He pulls Mrs. McDonald's body from the freezer and places it on the table.

"Just a few things, not to much at all. Maybe you will be able to make sense of it all. After all you are the detective."

"Captain now," I declare.

"Oh right, right."

"Now what was it you found?"

"First I want to ask you a question. Did you say that this body was burned up in a house fire yesterday?" Jones questions.

"Yeah, that's right, why?"

"Well, I know how much you hate being wrong Captain. Unfortunately, these are one of those unlikely times. These bones are at least twenty-five plus years old." He states.

I flash a confusing look towards Jones as he takes a bite of his breakfast. That is just absolutely disgusting. How can someone be eating in front of a dead body that has a twenty-five year old stench to it. As he is doing that my phone rings. It is Jenni once again, but I ignore it. I am a little busy at the moment.

"Put that away," I state to Jones.

"What," he mumbles with a mouth full of food.

"I said put your food away. There has to be some kind of law against that near a dead body," I hiss.

"There is, but I am following procedures. I make sure I stay within the guidelines," Jones smiles.

"Of course, you are," I snare. "Now get back to the rest of what you were saying."

He lays his breakfast burrito down and then he washes his hand. As he puts on a new pair of gloves I sigh loudly enough so that he knows I am losing patience.

"I'm coming, I am coming," he states.

He approaches the body as so do I. He grabs the separated skull and hands it over to me. I immediately notice what he is trying to show me. It is a bullet hole located in the middle of Mrs. McDonald's head. The same way one of The

Chevy Killers does his victims.

"Is that what I think it is?" I question him just for conformation.

"Yes, sir. That is one hundred percent and no doubt about it a gun shot wound."

I give the skull a worried look, and as I do a flashback begins to happen.

It is the same as my dream that I told Mr. Challenger about. This time though instead of leaving the woman's body to burn, I save the woman in the fire. I don't call the cops like I should have. I instead shove the woman in the trunk and drive off. My vision has a break and then reappears with me pulling up to a warehouse, or at least that what it appears to be. My point of view then starts cutting Mrs. McDonald into pieces like she is now.

Notice I say point of view that last time and not just myself. I do so knowing because I am not capable of doing that to a innocent human being. Then a disturbing thought crosses my mind. What if I am still having the effects of Frost's poison from the island. None of the doctors were able to tell me what I was poisoned by because it didn't leave a trace. So, how am I suppose to know about what the long term effects are.

Of course, I am not certain of this. I did learn one thing though, that I am certain about after looking at Mrs. McDonald's body. That the group known as The Chevy Killers has been around a lot longer than what we previously thought.

~Chapter 51~

I HAVE BEEN trying all morning long to get ahold of James, but every time I get no answer. The last few times that I have called it has went straight to voicemail. So, I finally give up on trying to call. I instead am going to look for him back at the station. He must know about Sarah.

It's not like James though to ignore someone calls like this. I get that he is busy with taking over the new position and all, but that doesn't mean he has to flat out ignore me.

Maybe he is mad at me for some reason that is not known to me at this time. I still don't understand any kind of man, so there is no telling. I could just be over reacting about him not answering and it could be something so simple as he is following up a lead. I just simply don't know at this point in time.

It takes me nearly two hours to get back to the station. Slow I know, but I had to walk remember and that is something I don't do much of. That was another reason I was trying to call James is because I needed a ride.

Why not call a cab you might ask. Well, I did think about that too and then two reasons stopped me. First, by the time I had thought about that idea I had ran my phone dead from attempting to call James so many times. Which means even if he did call back I couldn't answer, now.

The second reason being that when I left the station in a hurry this morning I left my wallet, which had my money in it at the station. Therefore, I had no money at all for a cab in the first place.

When I reach the station I don't take a wasteful breathe or stop for a drink. Even though that sounds amazing right now at this moment. I instead scurry in a hurry around the station looking for James.

After about thirty minutes of looking the station down floor by floor I catch a little bit of information about where he is. They say that he is downstairs with Mr. Jones. At first I felt completely stupid because I couldn't believe that I forgot to look there.

I dart in a hurry all the way to the basement. When I get down there, there is still no James.

"Where is Captain Gibbs?" I questions Jones.

"Not sure. He just said he had to follow up on a lead and that was all."

Now that dumb feeling I had inside me has just amplified because I knew that he wouldn't just ignore me for no ordinary reason.

I grunt and then proceed to tell Jones, "Thank you."

I give up on this mission now. My shift is now ending and I still haven't got hold of him. He will contact me whenever he can, I guess. I just hope that it is not to late. Sarah is a string girl and I want to trust that she knows what she is doing, but I can't. I feel uneasy about not knowing her plan. That and I don't really think she gets what she is up against.

I make sure I grab my wallet this time and I call a cab. It takes ten minutes for the taxi to reach the front of the station. I get in and the driver is a black man with dread locks.

"Where to?" he asks in a Jamaican accent.

"Home," I reply swiftly, "Home."

~Chapter 52~

I UNLOCK THE door to my apartment. When I reach the inside I place my belongings, such as my purse and my keys to a car that I can't drive right now, in my hallway closet. I know its a little weird to put my keys in a closest, but it is easier for me to have everything in one spot when I leave in the morning, that away I don't forget anything. I kick off my shoes and put them in the closet as well.

I proceed to my bedroom and I strip down to my panties and bra.

On this certain day I am wearing a matching pair from Victoria Secrets set, that James had brought me.

I walk into the bathroom and start the shower. As the water warms up I slip into nothing, but my smooth skin. I hop in the shower and begin to clean myself. I feel the warmth of the water running down my entire body, cleaning all the dirtiness off of me.

I am about done when I hear my door bell go off.

"Hold on, I am coming," I yell.

I turn off the water and slip into my pink bathrobe in a hurry, hoping that it is James. I rush to the door without a thought of anything in my mind.

I smile as I open the door.

"Come on in."

The man at the door is dressed in a nice slick back suit. Almost a federal government official type suit. The man then enters my apartment.

"Would you like anything to drink?"

"No," the man answers.

I go to the fridge anyways and as I do so I hear a noise that pleases me. I hear the man unzipping his pants.

I feel him approach me long before his arms wrap

around me. If you know what I mean then you know the body part that I am talking about starts going up my bathrobe.

"All I want is you," he whispers me in my ear.

I try to turn around to continue, but he stops me. He shoves me over to the counter and bends me over it. He then begins to pound me harder with each stroke from behind. I let out an emotional moan every time he goes in deeper because it feels so good.

Yes, if you are wondering by now I am having an affair. I guess you would call it that. It is hard to call it an affair when you are not technically married.

James is a great man and I didn't mean for it to happen, but it did. This mans name is Steven Walker. I just met him last week and we have had many fun times already.

When we finish I receive a kiss and then he proceeds to leave. Which besides for the sex is the best part because after all of this I still do love James. This person though is just completely the opposite of James. This man feels my needs of a young woman and doesn't want to settle down so fast.

About five minutes after he leaves the door bell rings again. Maybe he is back for a round two I think to myself as I smile. I could really use one of those after the day that I have had.

I answer the door, but it is not Steven. A man in a clown mask is there in the spot that Steven once stood. He shoves me into the room roughly and shoves a piece of cloth over my mouth. Within seconds I fall to the ground and pass out.

~Chapter 53~

I SIT PATIENTLY in a glass room office, for Bruce to return with his boss. That is the bad thing about government agencies. They take forever unless it is a matter of national security.

After about forty-five minutes of waiting I finally see Special Agent Jackson walking my way. The other man is elder than Bruce, but he has that swagger to him that I can tell he is the boss man.

They walk into the room and the other man approaches me.

"My name is Jack Jackson. Absolutely no relations to Special Agent Jackson over there."

I already knew that because Bruce is white as can be, and Jack is black. I know that makes no difference in this time and age, but you can just tell in this situation they aren't.

"Nice to meet you, sir," I reply.

We all three have a seat and begin to talking about the huge topic in the room.

"So, tell me what you have found out so far," Jack questions.

"Not much yet, this was just brought to my attention yesterday, sir. I think you should know though that there is a detective that has peaked her interest into the case," I state.

"Who?"

"Jenni Green. She is a friend of mine. She was just being over protective friend when she was doing a back ground on Randy Rodgers. That is when she found out his true identity as Josh Myers."

"Good that will just be extra protection for you."

"I would like for her to stay out of this. Especially if he

is as dangerous as you guys say he is," I declare.

"This man has murdered five women. He is as dangerous as they come, ma'am. If we hadn't found out his location you would have been number six."

"Yes, I am aware of this."

"And you are sure you still want to carry this crazy plan out? It is one thing for a trained agent to go undercover, but I speak for Bruce and myself when I say we are not to comfortable about sending a woman with no field experience into a dangerous situation. As I am sure Special Agent Jackson has pointed out to you, we can not one hundred percent ensure the safety of you or your unborn child." The director of the FBI states.

"I clearly understand. I just want this bastard to get what he deserves," I respond.

"Fine. Then you have my approval for this mission to begin. I will have my secretary draw up all the paper work."

It only takes about a half an hour for these papers to come before. They are just saying that if I or the baby gets hurt or worse then we can't sue the government because we have been warned of the high risk of this mission. Within seconds of getting the paper I sign them as quickly as possible. I sign it so fast I can barely read the signature.

Soon after that Special Agent Jackson and myself leave back for my apartment.

When we reach my apartment he tells me he will be close at all times. If he isn't then someone else will be not far away. I nod my head to symbol to him that I understand and then I get out of the car.

I go to the level of my apartment and walk straight in. I then call Randy/ Josh and tell him that I am ready to go on our vacation.

And that is how my mission begins.

~Chapter 54~

I WAKE UP IN my truck that is parked in the shade hidden from Mr. Challenger's point of view at his office. I am here to find out why I have this troubling feeling deep down in my stomach.

He first tells me that his wife was murdered by Frost. I know every victim of Frost and I never seen her name before. Then there is the random house fire that has a twenty-five year old corpse in it, that is a victim of one of The Chevy Killers. The only connection between them both is my therapist, Mr. Challenger.

He doesn't look like a very bad guy, but then again they almost never do.

I still remember this look on a murderers face from one of my previous cases. It was about five years again and the killer had pulled out a gun and shot sixteen people at a local elementary school. Ten of which were students. The horrible person that was responsible for these cruel and pointless crimes was an eight year old boy.

The boy looked so innocent as we questioned him inside the interrogation room. That is probably why I almost choked to death when the boy point blank admitted to the murders.

"I don't know why you are asking me all these questions," he stated at first.

Which would be a proper question for any young kid to ask. He could had been confused as to why, especially after being through such a dramatic experience. The next part to his statement though erasers all of that.

"I killed them kids and teachers," he straight out says.

When we went to ask the most important question of why he did it, his answer was just as bad. He simply answered by saying I had a dream last night and when I woke up I wanted to do it. As he told my partner and I that his eyes filled with so much hatred.

So, my point being is you never know when or who a person will commit a murder.

On the outside Mr. Challenger looks like a nice, simple, caring doctor. On the inside though he could be a lying, crazy-eyed, murdering maniac.

My phone begins ringing again, like it has been all day. Once again it was Jenni, and once again I hit the red button, called the ignore button. I figure I would use that instead of the unfriendly language form. It's not that I don't want to talk to her. It is just simply that I don't have the time right now. I am on a stake-out, well sort of considering it is during the day. Even though it usually takes place during the night.

This time I turn my phone off so that there is no chance of my cover being detected.

About that time Mr. Challenger leaves his work place. I follow him closely all across town for hours. Nothing interesting at all happens at all. Maybe my hunch was wrong this time. It has been known to happen from time to time.

Finally, I pull off and go home, to avoid wasting anymore pointless time on a unreliable lead. That doesn't mean I am giving up on the lead completely. It just means that I am going home for the night and I will pick back up my work tomorrow.

~Chapter 55~

I BEGIN TO READ one of the two notes that are on my kitchen counter. *Went on Vacation with Randy. I will be back in about a week. I love you, Sarah.*

Glad to see things are working out good between them. It will be healthy for the baby. Which now that I have had a day to think about it I can't wait to find out what she is having. I am hoping for a grandson so that I can teach him all kinds of different boys things.

I never got that chance to do that with any of my children because Sarah was my only child and she is definitely not a boy.

If she had a girl though it would be easy for me to do things with her because I been through the process of that before.

Whichever way I am pretty damn exciting about it and can not wait for the big answer.

I pick up the second note laying on the counter.

Either call me or come to my apartment as soon as you read this, please. I have been trying to reach you all day. I love you, Jenni.

Of course she had a note like this. She thinks that since I ignored her all day that I am mad at her for no damn reason at all. Well, I am not, but now that she is acting like this I am starting to get a little upset. She has done nothing at all to make me mad so I really don't get why she gets that idea at all.

I guess I shouldn't have ignored her all day even though it was for a good reason. I will not ever make that decision again unless I am on my death bed.

I probably should try to call her and let her know that I am coming over to make up for my mistake today. I pick up my phone and begin to dial the number. It rings and rings until I reach her voicemail. This happens a couple times and after the fifth time of calling I just figure she is getting revenge and ignoring me.

I go take a shower and freshen up. When I get to her apartment I want to look nice and I am going to take her to a very proper dinner.

I finish up all the finishing touches and then walk out of my apartment to my truck. Before going to Jenni's I head back to the station just to see if she is there first.

When I get there Mr. Jones informs me that she was there earlier looking for me just hours before. He then proceed to tell me that she said she was going home for the rest of the night. That if he was to see me to tell me that.

I go to the other side of town where Jenni's apartment is. I decide to take the elevator so I can get to her quickly. Even though I ignored her all day I missed her very much.

I reach the level of the apartment complex that her place is located on and go straight to her door. I knock a couple times, but she never comes to the door. I don't even hear her approach the door.

Maybe she is just asleep is my first initial thoughts. So, I bend down and grab the spare key that she hides under the "Welcome" mat. I unlock the door and walk in. The lights are all out. Which must mean she has to be asleep.

So, I go to her bedroom to sneak into the bed with her. When I do though she is no where in there to be found. I immediately go to the light switch and flip it on. Just as I said before she is not there. He bed is still made and my face changes from excited to worried in a matter of seconds.

I dial her phone number once again. This time though I can hear her phone going off in another part of the house. I follow the sound to the closet by the front door. I open the closet door and dig into her purse. There her phone is and reads James calling. I place the phone back into her purse and go to stand up.

Before I close the door back I notice that her shoes are in

the closet. She doesn't have a lot of shoes like most women have. She just has the one pair that she always wears. Meaning that she has to be in the apartment somewhere because she is not the type to leave without shoes.

Or.... The trouble thought crosses my mind. What if she has been taken. I look around for no clues at all. When I find nothing I drive straight to the station and find another detective.

I have this detective file a missing person report on her. About thirty minutes after the report is filed out there is a call that the detective receives.

He said the person on the phone is only asking to speak with me. I give him a strange look and go to answer the phone.

"Hello," I answer the phone.

"Mikey."

"Travis, what do you want," I snare.

"You need to go back to detective Green's apartment."

"What did you do?" I yell into the phone.

"I didn't do anything James, I promise. I am really sorry," Travis says as he hangs up the phone.

My heart sinks down into my stomach, possibly even lower than that. I rush to my truck and take off speeding through town. I know it is illegal to have you emergency lights on when there is not a real emergency. Well, to that I say fuck it, at the moment.

I arrive back at Jenni's place and dart upstairs. That is the fastest I have moved in years. I look like a sprinter in the one hundred yard dash in the Olympics. Even though I am much slower than those men, but I am fast for my standards right now.

I don't worry about knocking nor getting the spare key. I instead kick open Jenni's door and run inside. I look around and find nothing, until. Until I walk into the bedroom and there she is.

She is cut into several different pieces and put back together with a puddle of blood surrounding her, just like my wife's body.

I have loved only three women in my life; Shyanne,

Sarah , and Jenni. Out of those three important women in my life, two are dead. I can't help, but to think that I must have some kind of curse on me. I am never meant to live that happy ever after.

~Chapter 56~

THIS SCENE FEELS all to familiar as I drive behind the hearse that is carrying my dead girlfriends body. The hearse comes to a stop at the same location that my wife was buried just about one year ago.

It is not in the same section, but close enough where I will just feel twice the pain today. I wish that Sarah could be here with me today, but I let her be on her vacation. I probably should have called her and let her know the news, but I will let her have some fun before I tell her best friend was just murdered.

I grab my side of the casket and begin the walk of shame towards her final resting spot. The preacher does his thing just as he introduces me to say a few words.

When my wife was killed I broke down and was not able to speak a word. I have that same feeling inside of me now, but I must speak on her behalf. She deserved that at least. In a way I got her father killed and now her. I owe that family at least that much.

I walk up to the front of everyone and clear my throat. I look over at the hundreds of people who have attended the funeral. Most of them are from the police community. I try to stand up tall because I am different now than last year. I am the leader of this community, now and must look strong to them. If I look weak then the whole police community will look weak.

"This year has been a tough year for our community," I start off. "We have lost one of our leaders and now we have lost one of the young talents. Jenni Green had the full potential of being the next great detective in our system. I was proud to call her my partner and my friend. May she rest in peace."

I step down and walk back to my seat. There are a few more people who come up and talk on Jenni's behalf. Most of them are family of course.

The entire service last about an hour and half. When we are finished I walk back to my car and sit there as I watch people leave the site. I can't hold it in anymore and the tears begin to roll down my face.

Moments later there is a knock on my window. I gather my self together and look out the window. It is Commissioner Book. I open my door as he steps back a little bit.

"Commissioner," I state.

"Mr. Gibbs, I am sorry about your partner. She was a great detective."

"Thank you, sir," I reply.

"I am going to need you to come with me please back to the station," Book declares.

"Why?"

"Just to debrief you."

"Okay," I state.

We go over to his car which is really no different than any other detectives car. I get into the back with the Commissioner as his driver begins to go back to the station.

When we get there we go into the interrogation room instead of a debrief room.

"Sir?"

"Just come on in, James. We just have few questions," Book states.

I nod my head in agreement. After all I have nothing to hide. Well, there is one thing and I am sure that it will be revealed within the next couple of minutes.

I walk in and sit in the chair that I am not use to. I am sitting on the criminals side of the interrogation table. I am use to being in the chair that the Commissioner is sitting in right now.

I always wondered who would question the Captain if he was ever suspect for anything. I guess I know now. I understand why I am being questioned though I would do the same thing. I am the victims partner. I could have information about the killer that I didn't even know about.

"Where we you on the night of November nineteenth of

this year?" the Commissioner begins.

" I was tracking a lead on a case that I thought was reliable to the Frost and Chevy Killers murders."

"And was it?"

"No," I respond.

"If we look in the logs will it be logged."

"No sir, it will not be," I sigh.

Truth is I took a personal day for the rest of that day. I was just so caught up in the moment that I was so sure this lead would plan out. I say this directly to the Commissioner. I can tell that he is disappointed in me when I give him that response.

"I however did tell Mr. Jones, the medical examiner, that I was going to be leaving to track the lead. He knew everything about the case. You can ask him and I am sure he will back up my story."

"I'll make a note of it," he states.

"Is that everything?" I question as I start to stand up.

"Not yet, please sit back down, Captain."

I give him a weird look, but I do what he asks. He flips his notebook and begins to interrogate again.

"I am going to be completely honest with you. We have found some unfortunate evidence that has tied you to the investigation."

"What evidence?" I question.

"Why is it when we ran a DNA test on the semen found in Jenni that it matched yours?"

I knew the bit of information I was hiding would eventually come out. Jenni and I never did tell anyone in the station that we were dating. In fact, the only people who knew that I was seeing Jenni was Sarah and Randy. A lot of people thought we did, but no one had confirmation that we did besides those two people.

I say nothing in response to the Commissioners question. I instead sit there speechless.

"James! I ask you a question," Book yells.

I still give him no answer. Not because I don't want to, but because I can't. I am not sure how to answer the question because anyway I think of saying it sounds disrespectful.

"The day that Jenni was found dead there was only one person who went up to her room. The desk clerk said that the man gave the name Steven Walker, but he swore on his dead mother's grave that the man looked exactly like you."

"This is crazy, Commissioner. Just ask Mr. Jones about the case."

"I already did. He backed up your story."

"Then what in the world is the problem, sir," I yell.

"He says you were not acting like yourself when you left here. He said that you seemed distracted. So, I am going to ask you one more time. Why was your semen found in Ms. Green?" he states.

"Because..." I sigh. I then cover my face and wipe my eyes.

"Because why?" He screams in my face as he slams down his fist.

"Jenni and I were a couple," I cry out.

As I announce the big elephant in the room, I begin to cry again. Not because I announced this, but because of the flashbacks that are running through my head right now.

Every memory of Jenni and I together are flashing before me. Even some that I didn't remember all that well until now. It is like a trailer of a movie of our time together.

The Commissioner sits back down in his chair and sighs.

"I am sorry for your lost, James. You should have told us about this."

"We was going to make the announcement next week," I answer.

Which is completely the truth. Jenni and I had just had a conversation about this a couple days before her death.

"You should go and get some rest. If we have any following questions we will be in touch. I am sure everything will be okay though," Book answers.

"You know where to find me," I tell him.

"Yes I do," he responds.

I then get up and walk out of the room. I get a ride by to my truck and then go back to my apartment to rest.

~Chapter 57~

I LAY THERE in the lazy chair talking to Mr. Challenger about my previous weeks activities. This is the only way I seem to get any information out of Mr. Challenger. I have been following Challenger for about a week now and still haven't had any luck on finding out if he knows anymore than what he says he does.

Still no luck though, and he hasn't let out anything else out in the therapist sessions either. I really starting to believe that Mr. Challenger has just been in the wrong place at the wrong time and is not responsible for anything surrounding his wife, or his mystery neighbor.

"Our session starts right now," Challenger states to break the silence. "How have you been doing this week?"

"Well, I lost a really good friend in the last couple weeks. That is why I haven't been here for a while," I answer.

"I am sorry to hear that."

"It's okay. Can I be honest with you about something though?"

"Of course, that is what this place is for. I hope you haven't lied about anything else," he replies.

"Well, of course," I laugh. "With all honesty you and the others that have told me that you are sorry when you really are not sorry. You just say that because you want the conversation to move on smoother. If you said nothing about it then you would think that I thought you were being rude. If you knew the victim though, then you would be truly sorry."

He writes it down on a piece of paper.

"That was an off the record thing."

"It actually isn't because with you acting that way I can tell you were closer than what you say you were. I guessing the victim was a woman and she was more than just a friend. Am I right?" he insist.

"Yeah, but I don't want to talk about it today."

"Okay, then what do you want to talk about Steven?" he questions.

"Steven? Who is Steven?"

"Oh I must be talking to James, today."

"Well, yeah of course. Who else would you be talking about?" I declare back with confusion.

He doesn't answer me, but he sure does go and write on that notepad again.

"I asked you a question?" I yelled. "Why in the hell did you call me, Steven?"

"Calm down, James. This is perfectly normal for a patience to feel like this."

"What are you talking about?" I question.

"Have you ever experienced unexplained black outs or you woke up trying to figure out how you got there?"

"A few times. What in the hell does that have to do with anything, doctor?"

"When you black out you don't exactly black out. When those black outs happen the version of you named James Gibbs loses control," he announces to me.

"What exactly does that mean?" I question.

"You have a disorder known as Multi-personality disorder. A disorder that normal requires either medication or you get locked up in an asylum so that we can help control the situation. You were able to keep it under control for this long and I won't lie that is impressive, but now you are beginning to lose it." I hear him say.

"What was the name you said that this so called personality is calling himself?"

"Steven Walker. I have met him a few times and I have to admit that he is the complete opposite of you. He has so much anger built up inside him. That and he likes to talk a lot," Challenger answers me.

When the name Steven Walker rolls off his tongue I immediately recognize it. That is the name that the receptionist said the mans name was that entered Jenni's apartment building that day she died. Which would explain why the clerk said it was me that went there that day.

"I need just a minute," I answer.

"Certainly."

I begin to walk out, but before I reach the door I stop and turn back around to face my therapist.

"What would recommend that I do about this?" I question.

"I advise that you you admit yourself for help until you get this back under control," responds Challenger.

I nod my head in agreement and tell him that I will be right back. Seconds later my phone goes off and it is the station.

"Detective Gibbs speaking."

"James, this is Jones. Did you find out anymore information on the body in the lab?"

"No we been waiting. I told you that."

"I meant about the results about the DNA we found."

"What do you mean?" I question.

"The DNA results came back on Amy McDonald. The results came back without a match to any Amy Mcdonald. They match that of a Mary Frost. I did a little digging and that is the wife of former killer, Scott Frost. I told you this the other day," he states.

He tries to say more, but before he can I hang up the phone and run back inside. I don't worry about waiting for the receptionist to let me go back. I flash my badge and go straight back. When I get to Mr. Challenger's office he is no longer there.

"Where is he?" I yell.

"I don't know. He just said that he was going out. That he didn't know when he would be back," the receptionist answers.

"Dammit," I scream in rage as I punch the wall.

I pick up the phone and call the station.

"Put an APB out for Mr. Challenger," I yell to Jones.

~Chapter 58~

THE LAST WEEK has been crazy around the station since I put the APB out for Mr. Challenger. We still haven't had any luck finding him. Which makes me think that he has left town when he found out that I was interested in him.

The only weird thing about that though, is that I only spent about five minutes outside on the phone. So, if that is the case he knew about the findings of Mrs. Frost before I did. Which leads me to believe that Mr. Challenger has someone on the inside. If that is even his name in the first place.

Enough of that today though, because it is Friday and I am on my way home for the weekend. I normally don't take many weekends off, but from time to time I will. Especially, now that I have no life at home.

I took this weekend off though, because Sarah, Randy, and my grandchild are coming home today. I can't wait it has been two weeks rather than a week. Randy had called and said that they won some kind of sweepstake down there for an extra week. Which is great because it gave me an extra week to prepare how to tell Sarah that her best friend is dead.

I reach my apartment and go straight in. Sarah is not home yet, so gives me a little time to prepare dinner for them when they get home.

It doesn't take me long to stop that because I hit the voicemail button on my home phone. There was two boring messages over nothing, then there was one bill collector, and the final voicemail was from Randy.

He says that they are staying another week. Something about his parents bought them a wedding gift and let them stay down there another week.

My heart sinks because don't get me wrong I am glad that they are having fun. It's just that I miss her and I really need to talk to her about Jenni.

I hop in the shower to clean up. I put on my pjs because there is no need to get all freshen up. It is a Friday night and I no longer have a girlfriend and my daughter is not here.

I instead going to stay in tonight drink a few beers and

watch a movie on *Netflix*. I hit the couch and turn the television on. I flip through all the movies, but I stop on a tv show. I am sure that you can guess which show it was, but if you one of those people who haven't figured it out, it is the show that Jenni and I use to watch together, *Arrow*.

I begin to watch the show and the entire first three episodes of season one I begin to cry, because all of the memories of Jenni laughing and smiling during the shower. Then there is the first night we made love, we were watching this show.

I probably should have turned this show off about after the first ten minutes. I can't though for some reason. It is like I am in a complete stand still from shock. The show just keeps playing on and on.

Before I know it the first season is over and the birds are chirping outside. I take a quick glance outside and see that the sun is coming up. I can't believe that I stayed up all night watching this and bawling my eyes out.

On one hand I feel depressed. Then there is the other hand that I feel accomplished because I stayed up all night for the first time in forever. I feel like a twelve year old boy the first time that he stays up all night.

I walk to the kitchen and fix me a bowl of *Fruity Pebbles* before season two starts. I pour the milk in my bowl as my door bell rings.

I look at the digital clock on the stove and it reads, 6:21 A.M.. I am not expecting anyone at this time. Maybe it is Sarah, I think to myself as I begin to smile.

I rush over to the door, and immediately open the door. When I open the door I expect to see a pregnant daughter and her finance in the door way. Instead I see a black man in a federal type suit.

"Um, I think you have the wrong apartment," I declare as I begin to shut the door.

"Mr. Gibbs is it?"

I open the door back up all the way, and give the man a weird look like who the hell are you?

"Who the hell are you?"

"I am Special Agent Bruce Jackson. Is your daughter

around?"

"No, she is on vacation with her finance still," I state.

"If you hear from her, please, notify me immediately," he responds while handing me a card.

"What is this about?"

"I can't discuss this."

"I am her father and I would like to know what is going on. I can tell you are FBI by the way you dressed. And by the way you are acting my daughter is in trouble."

"Your daughter went on an undercover mission with her finance to Florida. She was suppose to be gone only a week, and now she has been gone three weeks. We have lost contact with her and we fear the worse," he answers.

"Were you not following them?"

"Yes, but we lost track of them. Mr. Rodgers is not who he says he is. Does the name Josh Myers mean anything to you?" he questions.

"Yeah, that is Randy's cousin."

"No Josh Myers is Randy Rodgers and he is a murderer. It is important that we find your daughter immediately. Has she tried to contact you?"

"No, Randy or Josh, or whatever his name is the only one who has been calling. Please come in. I want to hear more about this case," I insist.

He accepts my offer and comes in the apartment. He begins to give me details and tells me that Jenni knew about it. He said that the day she died she was trying to call me and let me know what was going on, but I wouldn't answer.

That would explain a lot as to why she called so many times that day. What if Randy/Josh killed Jenni and I could have protected her if I just would have answered the phone. Her blood is on my hands. What if Josh/ Randy is part of The Chevy Killers.

I discussed my part of the case with the Special Agent and he assured me that Mr. Multiple names is not part of The Chevy Killers. He also offered a hand in our investigation, but I respectfully decline. I told him though if the case goes cold I might need help later. He agrees with me an understands my point of view.

Most Federal Agents are dicks. They are always trying to push themselves in someone else case. Even when you tell them no they insist and push themselves to the top level. Then when the case is solved they take all the credit. Not Mr. Jackson though.

About that time I hear a bunch of cars pulling in. I look out the window and they are CPD. I am confused as to what is going on.

"Captain Gibbs," Jackson announces.

"Yes?"

"Please, don't try to run. You are completely surrounded."

"Why would I run?" I question.

"Because we know the truth, Gibbs."

"About what?"

"The people that you have been murdering," he announces.

"This absurd. I haven't killed anyone, but Frost on the island. Whatever this is I am being framed," I state.

"James Michael Gibbs, place you hands behind your back. You are under arrest for the murders of several different people."

"No, I didn't do anything," I yell.

"Save it for everyone else. I don't have time for you bullshit," he declares back.

We walk outside to the squad of police.

"Here is your Chevy Killer," he announces to the Commissioner.

He then shoves me into the back of the cop car as I watch all of the community watch me ruin my reputation, for something I didn't do.

~Chapter 59~

WE START DRIVING AWAY from where I just got arrested from. There is just an ordinary officer driving me to the station which I am a little bit surprised by considering the FBI is involved. They would have normally drove someone accused of these crimes themselves. That is just the kind of people though.

I know I said this about Special Agent Jackson though to because I thought he was different. I was obviously wrong because all he was doing was playing me. He was trying to get in close to me so that he could go in for the kill. I wasn't expecting to be arrested though , on such bull shit.

I really can't believe that they think I have been doing all of these murders. This is absolutely crazy talk. They are just getting desperate because they have nothing on the case. My semen that they found inside Jenni is the only lead they have and they going to pin it all on me even though I told them that we were seeing each other.

They probably thought that I was just lying and trying to cover my ass. Little do they know that I was telling the truth.

When we are about three miles away from the station the officer looks into his rear view mirror at me. I couldn't believe that I didn't notice who he was before. Hopefully you remember that story I told you once before about that cop who punched the suspect that had been causing the department so many problems and that had been fired. Well, right now he is driving the cop car and he is in complete uniform.

"You?" I say.

He says nothing, but continues to look back at me every once in a while.

"Why are they arresting me?"

"You know why, Captain."

"No I really don't. You must have heard of all the things they are accusing me of. You know what kind of man I am and you must know that I didn't do anything," I insist.

"It doesn't matter what I think sir," he replies.

"But you feel the same way about it as I do. So, tell me what they have on me. "

"I would tell you if I knew honest, sir. I know nothing though. When the FBI got on the case they left everyone out except the highest people in the station," he tells me.

I feel disappointed, but I know that he is telling the truth.

"For what it is worth I really did try to save your job back then," I tell him.

"I know you did. You must be quite though, we are about to pull into the station," he responds.

I say nothing, but I do nod my head to agree with him. I don't want to get him caught up into all of this, so I must.

We pull into the parking lot of the station. The officer has to honk his horn to make the press scatter like the little rats that they are. They must have already labeled me on the television as The Chevy Killer or they wouldn't be here.

"Great," I murmur to myself.

The officer stops the squad car and gets out. He then proceeds to walk over to my door and he opens it. He pulls me out and we walk through the crowd of rats to the front of the station.

He pushes open the door and we walk though the threshold. When we walk in the entire station of my former workers are staring at me.

As we walk by them all I hear is whispers of "Liar, trader, or murderer."

The officer takes me past them, but I can still hear the echos of the whispers. He takes me into the interrogation room and then cuffs me to the table.

"Is that to tight?" the officer questions.

"No," I tell him

As soon as I respond to him, Special Agent Jackson and Commissioner Book walks into the room.

"Make sure those cuffs are on there good," Jackson states.

"They are," the officer responds.

He then walks out of the room and Jackson sits down.

Commissioner Book stands up in the corner. I never knew that the commissioner would ever take a back seat to anyone. I never thought that I would be arrested for being a serial killer either, so I guess everything is possible.

Jackson slams down a file and then looks up at me.

"Would you like to admit what you have done and save us the trouble."

"No, because I didn't do anything wrong. I was sleeping with my partner and that is it. That isn't a crime, it's just not fond of. What you should be doing is going to find that Randy/Josh man that has my daughter. Unless that was a lie as well," I yell.

"No Mr. Gibbs that was the truth. Your daughter really is missing. I would love to have all of my attention on that, but I can't because her father is a serial killer. So, save us the time and admit to what you did so I can go find your daughter. You at least owe her that," Jackson exclaims.

"I am telling you that I didn't do anything. When you find my daughter she will confirm that she knew that Jenni and I was dating."

"We are not worried about your relationship with Ms. Green. If you guys had a relationship then fine, but that doesn't explain why you semen was found in Ms. Johnson, Mrs. Mickleson, and Mrs. James. So, stop playing with us and tell us why you did it," he states.

I sit there trying the silent treatment. Well, not completely there are a thousand things going through my mind right now. Like why did they find my semen in them? I never ever slept with these women so why am I being accused of it?

"We will find out why you did this. It is just a matter of time," he states as he stands up.

"Would you like a soda or anything?" The Commissioner says as they begin to walk out of the room.

"Yeah."

"That probably is a wise choice considering you will never have one again where you are about to go," Jackson laughs.

They proceed out of the room and leaving me to myself

to think. Most of the thoughts that crosses my mind is what am I going to do if they do send me to prison. I would be an ex-cop murderer and in prison. I would surely have the worst time in there, far worse than any other prisoner. After about five minutes of thinking of all terrible things that might happen to me in there, another thought crosses my mind. Well, not much of a thought just a simple word; *escape*.

~Chapter 60~

I CAN'T JUST simply escape. Then that would make me look guilty. They keep finding more evidence against me and even if I am innocent, like I know I am, I could still be found guilty. It wouldn't be the first time an innocent man was found guilty. The way things are going right now I will be the next victim.

I must escape then. It is the only way I know how to prevent myself from going to prison. I think about it for a little bit longer, and ultimately decide that I am going to go through with it.

"Hey!" I yell.

A few minutes later the Commissioner walks into the room.

"What?"

"I have to take a piss. Am I still allowed to do that?" I question.

"Yeah."

He then walks over and uncuffs me. We proceed out of the room and walk down the hallway to the bathroom.

"Don't be long," he declares.

I snare a look at him because I won't be long at all in fact. I walk into the bathroom and to my luck my plan is going to take even faster than what I thought.

I thought I was going have to wait for someone else to come in after me, but luckily there is already another cop in the room.

I slowly act like I am walking into the stall, but quickly walk in the other direction to where the cop is taking a number one. He isn't paying attention to me at all and that is going to make it much easier to do what I am about to do.

I slowly approach him and take the cuffs and wrap them around his neck. I squeeze until the officer passes out and falls to the floor. A silent takedown so that the Commissioner didn't hear.

I quickly reach the for the knocked out officer's gun and then stand back up. I move slowly over to the door and creak it open to see if the Commissioner is still there. Sure enough he is so I must think of something else. I sit there patiently for a moment and think about my next move. I can't take to long because then the Commissioner will come in before I am ready.

"Commissioner, come here quickly!" I yell.

As I yell for him I hide behind the door. Seconds later in runs Book. He notices the passed out cop laying on the floor. He quickly turns to run out, but stops because I have a gun pointed towards his head.

"What are you doing, James?" Book questions.

"I am innocent and you guys are trying to pin this on me. I am doing what I have to," I state.

"Come on, Gibbs. Think about what you are doing. This is making you look guilty as hell."

"I am not guilty, but you are not leaving me without any choice. Now put you gun on the ground and walk over here to me," I state.

"If you do this you will not be able to go back from this," he tries to tell me. He then places the gun on the ground and starts to walk my way.

"I really am sorry," I tell him

I wrap him up in a choke hold, not one like the other officer. This one is not as tight as the other one. I know it will work though because I have the gun pointed straight at his head.

I walk out of the bathroom and start going towards the exit. I am close and think I will not have to do anything to stupid when I hear someone call out.

"Hey, you stay right there."

He then calls in back up on his radio. Within seconds dozens of cops and FBI agents are surrounding me.

"If anyone moves I will shoot him. Don't test me," I yell.

"Put down the gun Gibbs," Jackson says back.

"I am innocent and you are putting the fall on me. You haven't even done a full investigation," I scream back with anger.

"That doesn't matter now," he says back.

I walk backwards slowly and everyone parts ways just as I knew they would.

"If you follow I will shoot him, I promise," I state.

I walk out of the front door the station and walk out to one of the squad cars. When I almost reach one I am stopped by the officer who drove me to the station.

"Back up," I yell.

"I am here to help," he declares.

"How?"

He says nothing, but he walks towards me. I want to back up because he could be lying. Something in his eyes though are telling me that he is telling the truth.

He gets to me and immediately lands a direct blow to the Commissioners head.

"What are you doing? That was my only leverage," I answer to him.

He says nothing once again just like in the squad car. He then turns my way and then lands the same blow to my head. I fall quickly to the ground and my eyes roll in the back of my head.

~Chapter 61~

TWO WEEKS AGO...

I WAKE UP IN my bed right beside Randy. I lean over give him a kiss on the cheek and then proceed to the bathroom. I lock the door behind me and turn on the fan in the ceiling, so that I will not be heard.

Before closing the door I look behind me to make sure that Randy has not woke up yet. Luckily for me he still is sound asleep like a baby when they are knocked.

I go over to the toilet and sit down. As I do so I grab my phone from my pocket and begins to *Facetime*. I wait for few minutes as it attempts to connect. Finally, it does and an African American, Special Agent Jackson's face appears.

"Any more news yet?" he questions immediately.

"No, but we are staying an extra week so I am sure I will find something out," I reply.

"Let me know as soon as you do," he states.

I have no chance to respond when Randy starts beating on the bathroom door.

"Why is the door locked? And who are you talking to?" he double questions me.

I quickly hang up the phone and delete the conversation. After doing so I place it back in my pocket and go back to the door.

He has beat on the door a couple dozen times now before I unlock the door finally. When I do he storms in looking around.

"Why was the door locked?" he yells

"I was using the restroom."

"Then why were you on the phone?"

"I wasn't and even if I was why would it matter? I can talk to whoever I want," I snare back.

He snatches my phone from my hands and begins to go

through it.

"Find anything interesting on it?" I say as I try not to laugh because I already know the answer is no.

He grunts and then walks into the other room.

"Why are you being so defensive, down here?" I ask.

"You just hear things on the news about the horrible things that happen down here all the time. I am just making sure that it's not going to happen to you is all."

"So, you go through my phone," I yell.

"You never know when an innocent looking person gives you their number. Then you start texting and they turn out to be a crazy person."

The thought that first comes to my head is that he must be describing himself. I think better though, and decide to keep my mouth shut.

A couple minutes later after all the tension past he goes into the bathroom and I go to the kitchen. I pour myself a glass of milk and then yell throughout the house without thinking this time.

"Josh, would you like anything to eat."

I cover my mouth trying to catch the words and put them back in my mouth. It's to late though they are already out there. He doesn't answer me though. So, maybe he didn't hear me and that is a really good thing. That idea changes, though when he comes to the room that I am in.

"What did you call me?" he states.

"Randy?"

"No, you didn't you called me Josh. Now why would you do that?" he snares.

"I honestly called you Randy, honey. Why in the world would I call you, your cousin?" I question him back.

"I guess I am just hearing things. I am sorry babe," he states as he kisses me on the cheek, "What did you need though?"

"I asked if you wanted anything to eat is all," I state.

"Yeah, I was going to run and go get something, though."

"It's okay, I will go do it myself. I am wanting some fresh air anyways," I try to insist.

"Honey, we are staying at a beach house. All you have to do is go outside on the beach," he teases.

"I know, I just want to get away from the house for a little bit is all."

"Fine." He sounds irritated.

I go and grab my shoes from the closest and place them by the couch. I then go to the bedroom to take a shower. I have this pet-peeve about going out in public and not showering.

Minutes into my peaceful moment, Randy tries to come in with me.

"What are you doing?"

"What does it look like?"

I huff and just go with it. When we finish and we begin to get out of the shower, I feel a push from behind. Well at least I think it was a push. It could have been him trying to catch me. I doubt it for some reason though.

I fall either way and crack my head on the side of the toilet. I am knocked out from it.

When I wake up though I am not in the bathroom no longer. I look around and it appears that I am in the basement. I pay a little more attention and I notice that I am tied up to chair and there is something over my mouth. I struggle to look at my mouth to see what it is. It is a grayish color, which means more than likely that it is duct-tape.

Seconds later, I hear footsteps coming down the basement stairs. In shorter time I see Randy/ Josh appear. I try to speak or yell whichever I could, but nether is heard because of the duct-tape.

He walks over to me with evil in his eyes. He rips of the duct-tape and laughs as he does it.

"What the hell?" I yell at him.

"Don't act surprised. You know to much about me," he states.

"What are you talking about?"

"You know what I am talking about."

"Then why are you doing this," I question.

"Because I can," he laughs as he puts the tape back over my mouth. He says nothing else and walks back upstairs. I hear him slam the basement door shut. Moments later the lights turn off, and I am left with my thoughts in the complete dark.

~Chapter 62~

I AM NOT SURE how long I have been locked up for sure. As I watch out the little window in the basement though, I have been down here in the basement for ten days now.

Another way that I have kept count is by the amount of times I get feed. I only eat once a day and if I am lucky the bastard upstairs brings me something to drink about three times a day. Just enough to tease my thirst is about it. As the days go on it gets harder each day to yell at him for the stupidity and craziness that he is performing.

"It's 8:32 A.M. on March 23rd. The skies are cloudy and the weather channel is calling for storms." I hear the radio broadcaster announce from a radio upstairs.

March 23rd, March 23rd, I continue to say over and over again. Trying to think of what that number meant to me. After saying it about fifty times it dawns on me. That is the date that Randy/Josh has killed all of his victims on.

I struggle around in the chair and try to free myself as the thought crosses my mind. This can't be it. This can not be the way my baby and I are going to die.

I hear movement coming from upstairs and it is approaching the basement door.

"Oh great," I tell myself.

I know what that noise is already. It is the boots that belong to Randy smashing the floor louder the closer he gets to me. The lights flip on as I am blinded by them and moments later there he is standing before me.

He has a tray with him like he does everyday at this time. He removes my tape and places the tray on my lap. I look down at is and notice it is the same thing that I ate yesterday.

I look up and spit into his face. He responds by back slapping me in my face. Blood drips down my lip.

"I am not going to eat this. If you are going to kill me today, then you better give me a better than this." I laugh as I turn my head back towards him.

I notice something though, that is different than the other

day when he brought me a tray of food. Most days he brings a plastic fork, but not today. No, today I get a a real fork.

"Nevermind, I will just eat this," I state.

"Good, because you weren't getting anything else," he declares.

I wait for him to leave and then I begin to eat first. I eat faster than normal even though it hurts me. He only gives me about fifteen minutes to eat, so I must hurry. It usually takes me the entire time to eat and I am still now done, but not today.

Today, it only takes me fives minutes. That gives me ten minutes to put my escape into plan. I wasn't planning on escaping, but by him giving me a fork he has given me a chance to.

I dig the fork into the tape that holds my hands. I quickly untie it and then go to do the same to the tape around my legs. When I am free I try to stand up as fast as I can. It is hard to do so because I am so weak from the lack of food and water.

Every step I take though I gain my strength back it seems like. I have to move gently that away he doesn't hear me walking up the steps. When I reach the top of the steps I throw an object down the steps that makes a loud noise.

Seconds later I hear Randy running towards the basement door and when he opens it I take the fork from my tray and stab it twice into his neck.

I take off running out of the beach house and run straight to the car hoping the keys are in there. I know my luck and should have known that it wouldn't be.

I run back inside to look for the keys, but can't find them anywhere. I would have just ran down the street, but the beach house is no where near anyone else.

I scramble around the house looking for the keys, but I can't find them. Then the thought of where it might be crosses my mind and I hate the thought of it. I must do it, though if I want to get out of this dreadful place.

I walk over to where I stabbed Randy in the neck, but he is no longer there. I look around and notice there is a blood trail going away from the crime scene. There is a a phone laying on the ground where he use to be laying.

I think nothing of it I just dart for the phone and immediately grab it. I dial Special Agent Jackson's number and then wait for him to answer.

Finally, he answers and I am so happy to hear him say, "Hello."

"It's Sarah, help." That is all I get out.

I have the phone slapped out of my hand by Randy. I stand up scared to death.

"What are you doing?" he states.

"You are scaring me, Randy. Please stop."

"Who did you call, and don't you lie!" he exclaims.

"The FBI. They will be here in minutes. So, you better let me go," I yell back at him.

"You are a lying bitch. Why in the world would you be calling the FBI," he declares.

"Because they know about the women that you have killed, Josh." I make sure I say the Josh part with anger in my heart so that he knows that I am telling the truth.

I know that he knows I am by the expression in his face. He reaches back and slaps me over and over again until he beats me to the ground.

When I fall he begins to land kick after kick to my stomach and my baby. I yell out in pain. I feel as everything is coming to an end as I begin to black out.

My vision is becoming blurry, and the pain stings worse every time. Right before I completely black out from lose of blood I see the front door being busted open. I also see Randy taking off running and then being tackled to the ground.

A face appears in front of me and I swear it looks like Special Agent Jackson. I have no chance to really tell because he is speaking, but I can't hear what he is saying. Then I completely black out.

~~~~~~~

My vision comes back in the back of the ambulance and Mr. Jackson is standing over top of me.

"What happen?" I struggle to say.

"We got him Sarah. We arrested him and he is in police custody right now," he declares.

An instant relief covers my body, but there is also the sick feeling still in my stomach. I then think about my precious baby.

"What about my baby?" I try to scream.

"You baby is completely fine," The EMT butts in.

A happy laugh comes out of my mouth as happy tears roll out of my eyes. I am so happy to be free of my crazy baby daddy.

"Does my father know that I am safe?" I question.

"There is something that we need to talk about your father," Special Agent Jackson states.

~Chapter 63~

I OPEN MY EYES and I am in an unfamiliar place, well sort of. At first I don't notice it, but when realization hits I do realize I have been here before. I am in the bunker of the island that Frost put me on before.

"Not again," I whisper to myself.

I am tied to the same chair that I had to use a blow torch to burn that tape out of my mysterious father, Richard Carr, arm.

I struggle around to free myself, but the ropes won't budge. A few minutes later the bunker door opens and in walks the officer from the squad car.

"What the hell is this and why am I back in this damn island?" I yell.

He says nothing, but he goes to a sink and pours some water into a glass. He brings me over the glass and lets me drink some of the water.

"Thanks, but like I asked what is going on?"

"Don't you know?" he responds.

"Not really," I say back.

"You will find out when they get here," he states.

"Who?"

"The people who recruited me. Well, at least the ones who I have been helping. The actual person who recruited is sitting in this room with me."

I look around just to make sure there is no one else in the room. When I find confirmation that we are the only two in the room I give him a dirty look.

"What do you mean I recruited you?"

"Well, it wasn't exactly you. It was your alter-ego, Steven Walker. Pretty fun guy to be around when you get to know him. Something you completely are not. Steven is the one who helped me out when you turned me in for assaulting that criminal," he states.

"I only turned you in so that you could have a case to defend yourself," I say at first then realize that he brought up my alter ego thing. "And how did you know about my alter ego?"

"Hold on I will be right back. Then we will start from the beginning."

He walks out of the room and moments later comes back with a chair in his hand. He sits it down in front of me.

"Here we go."

It was two days after I had gotten fired and was extremely pissed off. I went to Wal-Mart and bought a punching bag with my last check. I was practicing to pound your face in.

That is when I hear my door bell rang. I went to it and when I did answer it was you. Well, at least I thought it was you.

I asked you why you were there and then you proceed that you weren't the same man you were a couple days ago. At first I really didn't care and I did exactly what I practicing for.

I quickly started swinging and you started swinging back We fought for about thirty minutes until I got you in a choke hold and made you tap.

You told me about the team that you had set up and that you wanted me to be a part of the team. You said that my anger could be a very important tool to your team. You then proceeded to tell me about your alter ego.

"That is pretty much everything that happen. Besides me agreeing with your terms."

I sit there stunned at what I just heard. I have no memory of any of these. Then again, I have no memory of switching over to Steven.

"You said that Steven has a team?"

"That's correct," he replies.

"Do you know the other people?" I question.

"Of course, I do. After all we are all The Chevy Killers."

I nearly choke to death, but I can't because I need to find out who they are first.

"Who are they?"

"It's not that easy," the officer states.

"Come on," I insist.

"You will find out soon enough because they will be here any minute now."

He didn't lie because about the time there is a knock on the bunker door. The former officer goes over and looks through the peep hole. Seconds later he opens the door and three other men walk into the room.

"I will be back later," the former officer states to the three other men.

They wait for him to leave and then turn their faces to me. I recognize all three of them immediately. They are Travis Brown, Mr. Challenger, and Richard Carr.

"What the fuck!" I exclaim out loud.

~Chapter 64~

I SIT THERE in complete silence as the three of them look back at me.

"Are we going to just sit/stand here in silence," I yell at them.

They say nothing as they just laugh at me.

"What is so damn funny? I really am confused as to why Mr. Challenger is here."

Once again they don't answer me. Instead this time Challenger begins to remove a wig off his head and his fake mustache. When he gets done removing everything I notice that he is someone else completely different. Someone that I suspect all along that he was involved with, but I never believed he was actually Scott Frost.

"I-I-I killed you," I try to say clearly.

"When someone has an illness as you do they begin to see delusions sometimes. When you were on this island once before those test were set to put you back on the right track. You are the alter ego, not Steven," Frost says.

"That is why you don't remember most of anything when you were younger," Carr jumps in.

"Those flashbacks and dreams that you have are not that of Frost like he told you they are of yours as Steven, when you guys were little," Brown states.

I being to have a few of the flash backs again. Like the slaughter of the animals at the sink, and the house fire.

"The woman that was burning in your dream was not an accident that you dream. Those events really happened. That fire was the fire you set that killed your mother," Carr tells me.

"No that is not possible," I tell him.

"It did happen. When I put you up for adoption I was

protecting you. I knew that if I ran then they would have thought it was me not you."

The memories of everything before starts to piece together again. All of the memories that I had before on the island that Frost told me about I really did do it.

"So, how do you Frost play into this? Why are you here and why did you kill my wife along with your own?"

He turns his back to me and rest his arms against the sink. He falls silent and tries to not make eye contact with me at all.

"Hey, I asked you a question," I yell.

"Give him a second. This is a very touchy subject for him to talk about," Brown tells me.

"Touchy? He should have thought about that before he did that to both of our families," I scream.

"I didn't kill anyone," Frost jumps back in. "You did it as well. My wife died in a fire as well and the fire bug that did it was you."

"I never knew you before you came up on the data best."

"I was the one who adopted you the first time. I was the one who beat you all of those years. I beat you because you killed my wife."

That is not possible at all. Why would I do such a thing, I think internally. This is to much to take in. I am getting a terrible pain inside my head. I squeeze my eyes shut to block it from hurting so bad.

"So, you killed my wife for revenge, you bastard."

"No, I didn't do that one either. I gave you up to my best friend, Travis. We hoped that he could straighten you out, and he did. He was the one who made your good side, James Gibbs come out for a while. As many patients with your condition surfer from a relapse though, and this is exactly what happened."

Frost takes a deep breathe and looks on at me. He still hasn't told me what I want to know about my wife though. From the looks of it none of them want to tell me either.

"I want to know what happened with my wife, now," I yell.

"Think about it, James. All of the other murders that you commit think of your signature," Brown states.

"I don't know."

"Sure you do. You would like to watch the couples you killed have sex and then kill them. If you didn't pick up a couple then you would rape them yourself. Sometimes you would even join the couples. Then you would cut your victims in a black out sessions. When you would come back to them you would feel sorry for it and piece them back together."

"This still has nothing to do with my wife!"

"Yes it does, James. She was killed the exact same way you killed all your other victims. You found out that she was having an affair with the former Captain Green. That is why you ordered the hit on Green. You were starting to lose yourself and the only way we knew how to fix you is to let Steven out again," Brown replies to me.

I sit there and the tears begin to roll off my cheek because I can't believe what I just heard. I killed my own wife.

"What about Jenni? Did I do that one to?"

"Yes, she was beginning to piece it all together. Steven found out and killed her."

"So, I either pulled the trigger, framed, or gave the command to kill all of those people?" I question.

"Yes," they sigh all together.

As soon as that words rolls of their tongues I begin to have flash back of all twenty-eight murders that I completed.

They keep coming back and forth, over and over again until I can't take it anymore. I have an overload and fade into darkness.

I wake up and nothing is normal anymore. Frost, Brown, and Carr are all standing in front of me still. Something is not right though, I don't feel like I am in control at all. I get the feeling that I know why, but I am not sure.

It doesn't take long before I am sure though. That is when I see the three of them look at me with a curious look.

"Steven is that you?" Brown questions?

I want to say the words no, but my mouth won't move. I feel like I am trapped in my own mind. I am sure of it when my mouth finally rolls the words, "Yes."

I struggle to fight over control of my mind. The most intense battle that I have ever had in my life, but I am successful. I can't let the three fathers know. They cut the rope off of me and then I stand up straight.

"Welcome back," they say.

I smile at them because I don't want to give off any symbols that I am not Steven.

"We have work to do," Frost says.

"Yes we do," I reply.

They begin to walk out of the room as do I behind them. When we go to exit the room I notice a knife on the sink. I quickly grab it and stick it in my back pocket.

I wait for the three others to get back to the former officer.

"Feeling better Steven?" he questions

"Absolutely."

We walk throughout the island until we reach the dock where there is a boat parked. When we get onto the boat I take the knife out of my pocket and throw it to the ground.

I intended on using it, but I have a better idea when I see a gun on the boat. They go below deck and I quickly grab it. When I do I immediately go downstairs and point the gun towards them.

I don't hesitate, but instead I fire four straight shots at their heads. In order they drop like flies in a bug zapper. I walk over top of the bodies and say the words, "Game Over."

The weird thing though it was like second nature to do that. Well, I guess it would be a second person not second nature. My second person instincts kick in again as I throw the four of them over the edge of the boat and into the sea.

I go back to the wheel of the boat and take off away from the scene like nothing really happened.

~Chapter 65~

IT HAS BEEN a few weeks since the whole life changing events with my ex-finance. Special Agent Jackson told me about Josh's conviction. They gave him twenty-five to life, without the possibility of early parole.

Sounds like all good news, but then there is the information Jackson gave me about my father. He said that he was wanted for the murders of over twenty people, including my mother and Jenni. I am not sure now whether I was in a better position to be with Randy or my father. They both are sick as hell, but the question is which one is worse.

It doesn't matter one is behind bars and the other one is MIA. My baby and I are completely safe now from any evil son-of-bitch now.

Yesterday, I threw all of my father's belonging away. To be exact I threw them out the window and they fell into the dumpster.

I hear my doorbell ring and I go to check it not thinking. When I open it, of course I am in trouble again. It is my father. He pushes his way into the apartment.

"You can't be here," I say.

"I just need to grab a few things and then I will leave," he states.

"I threw your stuff away," I yell.

He goes straight to his bedroom and goes to his closest. In the top of it he grabs a bag that I didn't see. He unzips it and there is thousands of dollars in it.

"What the hell, dad?"

"Please come with me. You, the baby, and I can start over," he declares.

"I will never go with you," I snare.

He doesn't wait he just pushes past me and goes to the kitchen, goes to the cabinet and grabs a gun. He places it in the back pocket and takes off.

"Are you sure?" he tries to ask again.

As his back is turned I grab a knife.

"Yes."

He then turns and goes to walk out of the door. As he does so I raise the knife and I stab him in the back with it.

"Matches what you did to this family," I say out loud.

I watch as my father falls to the ground. I dart for the phone and call nine-one-one.

"What is your emergency," the operator states.

"I just stabbed James Gibbs. He is laying on my floor. Please hurry, I am not sure if he is dead or not."

"Help is on the way."

The phone clicks off and I turn back around to where the body was laying. Notice I said was, that is so because the body is no longer there.

I look around the room and see him no where. I decide to follow the trail of blood and of course it leads it right to him.

"What the hell was that for?"

"You killed my mother. What did you expect?" I yell at him.

"So, you stabbed your father?" he snares.

"Listen dad the cops are on the way. Please just don't do anything stupid."

This all feels way to familiar. Just a couple weeks ago I was involved with the same situation.

The bad thing though, he doesn't want to hear those words. I can tell because he strikes out at me. As he does so I hear a loud banging noise. My father begins to fall to the ground. I have to move over a step so that he doesn't fall on me.

When he falls he goes crashing into the glass table in the middle of the living room. There is blood spitting out of his shoulder where he was shot. A few seconds later a cop comes into the room.

"You are safe now. Ms. Gibbs," he declares.

"Is he alive?" I question.

The cop walks over to my father's body and feels his pulse.

"Yes, now please step back. Back up is on its' way," he suggests.

~Chapter 66~

"I SENTENCE YOU to twenty-eight life terms in the Chicago Prison. The judge announces throughout the court room.

I tried to claim that I was mentally unstable since that is what all killers do these days. Unfortunately, for me the therapist who said I was declared insane is now dead. I did it myself because he was part of my alter ego team.

The officer comes over and gets me from the room. I wait in the cell for hours before I see anyone. Finally, when they come to get me they put me in the back of the bus.

We drive around for a while until we reach the prison. They take me straight in and I do the normal routine; I speak with the warden, then get force to take the shower, and get dressed they take me to my new home.

"Open prisoner number 226408's cell," the prison guard announces into his walkie.

Seconds later the cell door opens and I walk in. I met my new cell mate, and it is someone that I am all to familiar with, Josh Myers.

That is the good thing about having money in prison. When you have it, you can almost arrange anything you want. When I first heard that I was going to be attending the same prison as Myers I felt this sensation go throughout my body.

When Myers notices me walking into the cell he completely freaks out. He tries to run out of the cell, but when he does the guard shoves him back into the room.

"Have fun," The guard states as he hands me a knife looking object.

"We will. I will make sure your payment is wired to your account by the morning," I declare.

"It better be."

He then walks away and I turn my attention back to Myers. I smile at him as I hold the object in my hand.

"I never would have hurt her, James," he cries out.

"Then why did you beat her? And my name is not James. It is Steven, Steven Walker," I exclaim to him.

"Come on. You have killed people to and you know that you can't control it," he pleads out.

"That might be. You just happened to attempt to kill my daughter. So, us both being serial killers and all, you must know that what is about to happen," I declare.

He runs to the cell door and cries out for help.

"Hey, no one is coming to help," I say.

He turns around with a scared look on his face. I don't wait any longer. I take the knife and start stabbing right into his stomach over and over again.

I wait until I see life leave his eyes, and then I drop him like a rock to the ground. The other inmates start going crazy as my list goes from twenty-eight to twenty-nine.

~Chapter 67~

A YEAR LATER....

"I WILL BE FINE," I tell Bruce as I get out of the shower. Yes, Bruce as in Special Agent Jackson. After everything that happened we stayed in touched, and about two months ago we got married. It was sudden, but I felt safe in his arms and I still do.

"I just don't think going to see your father is the best thing. It seems a little to early to be doing that don't you think?" He questions.

Yeah, he is right, it is way to early and I don't want to see him. He called however and said that if Grayson, my son, and I went to go see him today then he would never bother us again. He pleaded that he just wanted to meet his grandson once and that is all. Then he would be gone forever.

Sounds pretty good. I think I can sacrifice one day of hatred so that my son stays away from that monster.

"It will be fine. If it makes you feel any better you can drive me there. That away if anything happens you will be right there," I state to calm his nerves.

He nods his head to agree as I knew he would. He is so over protective and I don't blame him after everything I have been through.

"Well, come on. I don't want to be late," I lie.

We scurry out of the apartment and go to our car. I the gene trait that my mother did about luxury cars. I even bought the exact same car that she use to own.

We drive off and we pull up to the prison gates. As we do so I feel a cold shiver go down my spine, like the one you get when you have a bad feeling about this, Then again it could be that the last time I seen my father he tried to kill me.

Bruce parks the car and I tell him to stay out here even

though I know he is isn't going to listen. Surprisingly though, he does.

I get Grayson and proceed to go inside. I wait for about ten minutes when my father finally comes in.

"What do you want?" I snare.

"Wow straight to the point! I already told you what I wanted; just to met my grandson," he states. "Speaking of which, he looks like you. What is his name?"

"Grayson," I short answer him.

"So, Randy/ Josh is dead," he says.

"I heard."

"Well, I wanted you to know that I was the one who did it. I figured it would set you free of being scared all the time," he declares as if he is trying to say he did it for justice.

"The only person I am scared of is you father," I snare.

"I understand. Well, could you start coming to see me?" he questions.

"No. You will never ever see us again. You are dead to me. Do I make myself perfectly clear?" I yell.

He frowns, but I know that he gets it. And he should because I am telling the truth.

"Goodbye, Sarah-lou," he says as he gets up from the chair.

I do the same and I exit the prison. I go back to the car where Bruce is. I just sit there in silence for a minute until Bruce breaks it.

"Are you okay?"

"Yeah, I am fine."

"What did he want?"

"Absolutely nothing," I say back.

"Then what is bothering you, dear?" he questions.

I smile a huge smile and begin to say, "Nothing. I just for once in a very long time feel free."

"Good," he states as he reaches over and kisses me. "Now where to?"

"Home," I say softy," Just home."

~Epilogue~

TWENTY YEARS LATER...
    I PREPARE FOR MY visit as my palms are sweating like crazy because today is the day.
    I hear the buzzer for the door go off and in walks a six foot man, with blondish-brown hair. He is built like a line backer because that is exactly what he is. He plays in college for the University of Chicago. His name is Grayson Gibbs, my one and only grandchild.
    He has been coming to see me for the past two years and we have talked about everything. To be honest him coming to see me is the best thing in the world.
    He found out about me being in prison from a person at school. He told me that he went home crying and I told him to raise his head because Gibbs don't cry. That we are stronger than that. he naturally agreed because he knows that it is in his DNA.
    We don't talk much, but when we do he helps me out with regaining my humanity. He has even talked Sarah into coming to see me every once in a while. Of course, after all these years she is still mad at me. Even though she won't admit it.
    Those fifteen minutes are the fastest of every week. They help me though, get to the next week.
    As he begins to leave I tell him the words, "You know what to do."
    He nods his head and we separate in our different directions like every week. I walk slowly back to my cell and rest my eyes because the rest of the day is going to be long. I have pissed off several people in here and don't know how much longer I will last.

    About six hours later my cell door opens and Special Agent Jackson walks in.

"Pack up," he states.

"What?"

"I go you a transfer. So, come on," he declares.

I get up from my bunk and gather my belongings. I then follow him outside of the prison and into the back of his car.

We drive about twenty miles in complete silence. He never did tell me what prison I was being transferred to. So, I just ask him.

"Where am I being moved to?"

"You are not going anywhere!" he exclaims.

"What?"

About that time a truck slams into the side of our car. It is my truck ramming us. I would notice it anywhere. As soon as the truck hits us our car begins to flip, and flip, and flip. Finally, we come to a rest about fifty yards away from the initial impact.

Before I can gain my strength I see Bruce get up and come to my door. He drags me out of the car to the truck. He then throws me in the back of the truck. I try to sit up, but it is so hard to do.

Finally, I do though. When I do I notice the two people in the front seat. It is Sarah and Grayson.

"I told you papaw that I wouldn't fail you," he smiles.

"I knew you wouldn't," I answer him.

"Are you okay, dad?" Sarah questions.

"Yes, perfectly fine," I state and then look over to Bruce who is sitting beside me, "Thank you, Bruce."

"Please just call me son," he states.

I smile as I shake his hand.

"Now lets get the hell out of here before they come looking for us," I snare to Sarah.

"Sounds good to me. Did you make the arrangements, Grayson?" Sarah asks him.

"Yes, we have four tickets to China," he states.

I reach in the front seat and shake his shaggy hair.

"That a boy," I say.

Sarah then starts up the car and we take off into the sunset. I roll down the window and feel the fresh air.

"Roll that up," Sarah says.

"I want the fresh air. It has been twenty years."

"Soon enough you will have all the fresh air you want," Bruce smiles.

I roll the window back up and smile.

"I guess there really are two sides to every story," I say.

We all laugh and smile as we drive to freedom.

The End....

Printed in Great Britain
by Amazon